THE BARGAIN

"It is good," Traveler nodded, handing his knife to the chief. "Come on, girl. I hope you are worth it."

He seemed not entirely pleased with his bargain.

Pale Star's head was still reeling. The fact that she now had a different captor had not really reached her consciousness yet. Besides, that was insignificant compared to what she had just seen.

It was known among her people that the Elk-dog Medicine of her ancestor, Heads Off, was very powerful. It was supposed that part of its strength came from the strange substance from which it was made. Hard, smooth and heavy, it could be warm or cool to the touch. Looks Far had allowed her to hold it for a moment once.

Now, she had seen a knife made of the same material. She longed to know more about it. Where had it come from, and how had Traveler acquired it?

Pale Star

>> >> >> >> >> >> >> >> >> >>

DON COLDSMITH

BANTAM BOOKS
NEW YORK · TORONTO · LONDON · SYDNEY · AUCKLAND

RL 6, IL age 12 and up

*This edition contains the complete text
of the original hardcover edition.*
NOT ONE WORD HAS BEEN OMITTED.

PALE STAR

*A Bantam Book / published by arrangement with
Doubleday*

PRINTING HISTORY
Doubleday edition published February 1986
Bantam edition / December 1988

ISBN 0-553-27604-2

Published simultaneously in the United States and Canada

---

*Bantam Books are published by Bantam Books, a division of
Bantam Doubleday Dell Publishing Group, Inc. Its trademark,
consisting of the words "Bantam Books" and the portrayal of
a rooster, is Registered in U.S. Patent and Trademark Office
and in other countries. Marca Registrada. Bantam Books, 666
Fifth Avenue, New York, New York 10103.*

PRINTED IN THE UNITED STATES OF AMERICA

O   0 9 8 7 6 5 4

Introduction
by Ardath Mayhar
›› ›› ››

Very infrequently does a book come along that addresses the subject of the American Indian from a viewpoint that is untainted by the misconceptions and the biases of those Europeans who first encountered the tribes living on this continent. Even less often is there one that deals with the status and lifestyle of the Indian woman, which was seldom exactly what the prejudices of the European observer determined those to be.

Now Don Coldsmith is weaving an intricate tapestry of books that shows a living culture uncontaminated by the influences, customs, and assessments of the white race. The European artifacts that his Elk-Dog People possess have been few, so far, coming into native hands from the race that is slowly taking over a dominant position in America. In *Pale Star* we see the first of the Elk-Dog People to meet white men, face to face.

Europe, at the time of the westward expansion, had lived for hundreds of years with a concept that was imposed by the patriarchal religions originating in the

Middle East. Before that surge of expansion into the rest of Europe, which took place with the Romans, the Celts had lived lives of great equality between the sexes. The Romans, indeed, had a saying, "Don't kill a Celt—then you'll have to fight his wife!"

Queen Boadicea of Britain, warrior-queen and some-time-victor over Roman troops, was no fluke. In Celtic Europe, women owned and created property, were not enslaved by marriage customs, fought beside their men-folk, if that was their bent, and shocked the fanatics moving up from the desert countries by knowing them-selves to be no better and no worse than men. That trait was the target of a long-standing propaganda campaign among Christians and Jews (not to mention later Moslems) that culminated in the near-enslavement of women over most of the West, becoming noticeable in the Twelfth and Thirteenth centuries.

This was rigorously carried forward, there being in France at one time a law *requiring* any man who met a woman who walked with her head up and met his eyes to beat her into submission. By the time of ex-pansion into America, this attitude had acquired the validity of tradition (as well as the delighted accep-tance of males who were happy to remove a source of competition).

It is easy to see, then, why men who observed In-dian women working in the fields of the eastern tribes concluded that they were totally dominated by the men, who hunted and fished and left the hard work to their submissive spouses. They did not know, and if they knew they did not believe, that those fields and their produce were the possessions of those same women or that all material property, except for per-sonal clothing and weapons, belonged to women, who, in addition, provided the group of elders who chose the chiefs and could depose any of their choices who did not live up to their standards, replacing him with one who would come nearer to their requirements.

While this was not true in all tribes, variations of it occurred in a number of them. And even in those in which women did not choose the leaders, one must remember that a leader, to an Indian tribe, was not a king or a ruler. He was there in case of need or emergency, for most of the Indian people were very much autonomous, and nobody really gave them 'orders' in the sense that we know the term.

Women were listened to with respect in most tribes that I have encountered in my reading, and as in our own culture, it is more than probable that their husbands listened to them with attention when they offered advice.

This would have flown in the teeth of all that the white men had been taught. It would be interesting to know if any of the women among the Puritans and the Pioneers ever guessed what their menfolk never admitted, that their Indian counterparts were far more respected and valued than they were in their supposedly civilized context. Probably not—enslaved women dislike free ones, in the main.

In the eastern country, the growing demands of the whites for furs and deerskins did, of course, put a premium, in time, upon the prowess of the Mighty Hunter, for trade goods were the wealth that he could bring into the tribe. At that time, the influence of the women began to weaken. That, however, was a result of the impact of an alien society upon their own, not of any built-in sexual prejudice upon the part of the Iroquois or their fellows.

Those same Europeans, as they moved westward, noted each succeeding tribe as simply barbarians, never recognizing or understanding the interesting cultural and social differences among them. But they were people with real cultures and widely different customs. Some, indeed, rated women low on the scale of things, but many respected them, and all, whether or not they admitted it, relied totally upon the inventiveness and the work of women for any grace and comfort there was in their lives. Clothing, food, shelter, tools ... all of those were made by women from found materials, only infrequently aided by things for which they traded with other tribes.

Imagine being without any source of material possessions other than the woods, the land, the living plants and animals and the flints and stones, the waters and their denizens, and other naturally occurring matters about you. Think about having to create the tools you must use to make the things your family must have to survive. And then assess the importance of mere fishing and hunting.

When we meet Pale Star, she has been a member of the Rabbit Society of her tribe, that being the training group of small children who learn to hunt, to shoot, to trap, to swim, to do all the things that everyone, male or female, must know in order to survive in a world in which you must be able to help yourself, at need, without recourse to anyone else. So when she is captured by the men of the forest tribe, she is strong, she is skilled, and she is a fully effective person in her own right, not a female wimp of the sort our kind has seemed determined to produce, until recent years.

Her loyalty to the children captured with her is the sort that tribal cultures nourish. Her fatalistic parting from them is that kind which a harsh and unforgiving environment imposes on those living within it. But her determination to escape is strong and admirable, and her eventual decision not to leave the couple who have become almost like parents to her is equally worthy of admiration. She is a caring human being, and anyone who thinks that because Indians tended toward stoicism they felt nothing is, of course, mistaken.

Human beings do not differ radically from each other in their internal reactions to circumstances. It is only in their outward seeming that any difference is perceptible, and it is cultural conditioning, to a great extent, that determines what that outward appearance will be.

It is interesting to note that Traveler, who bought her from her captors, falls easily into the role of father to the girl. Even as she matures, and after his wife dies, it is most uncomfortable to him when others hint at a sexual attachment between the two. This is a human trait, which I feel sure must have been as common among native Americans as among Europeans, and perhaps it may have been even more often to be found. The Indians were not sex-obsessed nearly so much as those coming from the decayed warrens of European cities, and they had many other matters to interest them and keep them busy.

The differing menstrual customs among the tribes are mentioned here, and the primitive belief that a woman during her cycle was unclean and somehow dangerous is one to be found almost around the globe. Those who believe that it was a sort of punishment for being female to be banished to a special house will perhaps be surprised that the women in Coldsmith's Menstrual House are very happy to be temporarily relieved of duties and marital relations, even to the point of prolonging their stay past any real need. Think of the nightly headache among our own kind and you will see the kinship of women, whatever their kind.

This book is particularly interesting in that it moves this girl of the Elk-Dog People across a great deal of territory. She meets, along the way, a number of different kinds of people and customs and situations, even learning a language or two that she didn't know before. The mingling of the ways that she has encountered visibly enriches Pale Star, as she and her foster parents move up the country.

It is with the death of Traveler and her capture by Three Owls, the madman, that her strength of selfhood and of purpose is tested and found sufficient. One matter that springs immediately to the attention of the reader is the fact that she suffers no guilt because of her rape. It is enough that she is beaten and enslaved and mistreated and worked to exhaustion; she does not waste time and energy bewailing her sexual fate, as many white women in similar circumstances tended to do.

Guilt is the result of intent. There being no intention of wrongdoing on her part, she feels no guilt for what happens to her, and that is a far healthier thing than our culture has taught its own daughters. Attend any trial for rape in our modern 'civilization' and you will find that the injured person is often made to feel far guiltier than the criminal.

Among tribes that sold their women temporarily to travelers for their comfort and amusement, there was likewise no guilt. This was a way in which to acquire wealth, and I suspect that if such activity was the only way in which our own kind could further its prosperity it would be as common among us as it was among a few tribes of Indians. Indeed, prostitution as a profession was little known in that society, until the whites introduced it.

Being unencumbered by guilt, by weakness imposed by cultural requirements, or by general wimpiness, Pale Star survives her ordeals and goes forward, still interested in the world about her, still enjoying unusual scenery and colorful sunsets and flowers and animals and trees. This is a truly primitive trait, the ability not to look back and moan and groan over things that cannot be changed.

A modern American girl, even one with the physical stamina to survive what this Indian girl has done, would not, I think, come out (if she came out at all) with her spirit whole and her self-respect undamaged. We have divided ourselves too widely from the natural world, the quiet acceptance of the animal in pain and the unthinking knowledge that we must proceed with life, no matter what has gone before.

I do not claim, nor does Dr. Coldsmith, that the American Indian was some sort of saint or angel. These were people, just as you and I are people, with their own individual traits, from the insanity of Three Owls to the innate decency of Traveler. They had destructive habits among them that can make you shudder, and they had great ability and humor and much talent for living with the world as it is without leaving it irreparably damaged for the generations to come.

That, if nothing else, should make us think long and hard about our own ways and our own aims. Pale Star and her people, as well as those among whom she travels, may be far better role models than modern-day sociologists might think.

We may wish, before we are done, that *we* had learned some important lessons from these people whom our ancestors considered vermin and tried to wipe from the face of the earth.

—Chireno, Texas
March, 1988

Time period: Early seventeenth century, shortly after *The Sacred Hills*. No. 9 of the Spanish Bit Saga.

Prologue
>> >> >>

It was hot that year, in the Moon of Roses, when the People gathered for the Sun Dance. The lodges of the tribe, erected in ceremonial positions, were adapted for the unseasonable heat. Each lodge cover had been rolled up at the bottom to allow the breeze to blow through and cool those inside.

Spotted Fawn lay on her robes and looked out across the open space toward the camp of their allies, the Head Splitters. It was odd, she reflected. When she was small, the Head Splitters were her enemies. The alliance had been forced by the invasion of the Blue Paints from the north. It had been necessary for former enemies to join in stopping the invaders. Since that time, the two tribes had lived in harmony.

The pain came again, and the girl tensed involuntarily. She was tired. It had been long, this birthing. Something not quite right about the position of the child, she supposed. Blue Dawn, skilled as a medicine woman, said there was no problem. Dawn had been with her through the day, talking, encouraging, wip-

ing her face, or cooling her with a fan made of the tail
feathers of a red-tailed hawk.

"Do not push yet," her mother, Running Eagle, ad-
vised. "Wait until it is time."

Her mother had borne three children, of which Spotted Fawn was the youngest.

"But when?" the girl asked impatiently.

It was frustrating to wait. She took a deep breath
and relaxed again as the spasm passed. Several people
were walking from the Head Splitters' village, toward
the medicine lodge of the People. She could not see
the lodge from where she lay, but she could imagine it
in her mind's eye.

It was an open-sided arbor, roofed with brush. She
had watched the family of Yellow Hawk, the Real-
chief, bring the ceremonial buffalo and erect it in the
arbor. With head still attached, the skin was arranged
over a frame of poles and brush. Before this effigy, the
ceremonies of the Sun Dance would take place. There
were dances and prayers of supplication, thanks for
return of the grass and the buffalo. Individuals made
special vows, sacrifices, and offerings as the days passed.
Exhausted dancers dropped out to rest, and others
took their places, as the dancing continued without
pause for the five days of the ceremony.

Spotted Fawn wished that she could be there to
watch. It was always exciting. Their new allies, the
Head Splitters, had been much impressed by the Sun
Dance, its purpose was so clearly similar to their basic
customs. They had no Sun Dance of their own, but
since the alliance they had attended that of the People
by invitation.

Her thoughts were interrupted by another spasm of
pain. *Aiee*, it would be good when this was finished.
She wished, almost, that she were still a warrior-sister
in the Elk-dog society. Then, observing her vows of
chastity, she would be dancing now, perhaps, fulfill-
ing her function as a priestess of the warrior society.

But no, it was better this way. She had resigned her
office to marry White Hawk, one of the handsomest of

the young warriors. They had been extremely happy together. Hawk was a skillful hunter and kept their lodge well supplied. Now she would be proud to bear his child.

Only she would be glad when the birthing was over. She turned to look in the other direction, away from the camp to the southeast. Her Southern band, in its assigned space at the south edge of the camp, faced open country in that direction. The shadows of the hills were becoming long, the sky near earth's rim to the southeast dimming in the intensity of its blue. By chance, her eyes fell on a star, the first star of the evening. It was pale and white, barely seen against the gray-blue background.

Another spasm seized her belly, and this time she could feel something happening. There was a sudden shift, a movement within her. It was as if something turned, or was released. She could feel the infant descending, and there was no longer any decision about pushing. She had no choice. The involuntary contraction of her abdomen propelled the child downward. She choked back a cry of alarm.

With a gush of fluid the infant propelled into the world. Blue Dawn grasped and lifted the child, holding it head down to let the waters drain from the tiny lungs. The little creature seemed to sneeze or cough, filled its lungs, and made the lodge resound with its life-making cry.

"You have a girl child," Running Eagle said. "She is well formed."

Spotted Fawn was pleased. Her mother was an important woman in the tribe. In her youth, Running Eagle had led a campaign of vengeance against the Head Splitters that the People still remembered as Running Eagle's War.

The two older women cleaned the infant, wrapped it in a soft-tanned skin, and handed it to Spotted Fawn to nurse. The new mother smiled as the child sought the breast.

"Fawn? The child is here? You are all right?"

The voice of White Hawk came from outside the lodge. She knew the wait had been difficult for him also.

"Yes, my husband. Come and see her."

Instead of coming through the door, White Hawk knelt to peer under the rolled-up lodge cover. Spotted Fawn smiled a welcome. Over his shoulder she could see the star again. It was brighter now, rising and gaining strength as the darkness deepened.

"What shall we call her?" White Hawk was asking.

Spotted Fawn smiled in the dim twilight.

"Her name," she announced proudly, "is Pale Star."

1

>> >> >>

It was in her fourteenth summer that the events occurred which changed the life of Pale Star. There had been reason in her early childhood to foretell these things.

Spotted Fawn had always regarded the child as special, one destined for great things. However, such is the privilege of mothers. The growing child was alert, intelligent, and physically adept, and the elders of the tribe took notice of her quickness.

There was none among her peers in the Rabbit Society more thoughtful, and few more skilled at the games and contests. She was adept with the throwing sticks immediately, she could run like the wind and swim like the fish in the clear cold pools of the prairie streams.

These skills caught the attention of the elders, and the older ones remembered her grandmother Running Eagle. Not since the childhood of that one, originally called Eagle Woman, had there been a girl who exhibited such qualities.

With all this, the child was quiet and thoughtful.

There were none who spoke ill of her, for she gave no one cause to resent her. She was obedient and helpful to her parents, and a joy to them. She was their only child, as they had been unsuccessful in producing another.

There was one person who saw deeper into her thoughtful character. Looks Far, the medicine man, was her special confidant.

"Uncle," the child would say, "tell me of the Blue Paints."

Looks Far was not her uncle, of course. She used the term as a term of respect, applicable to all adult males older than oneself. However, they were related by blood. Both were descended from Heads Off, the hair-faced outsider, who brought the First Elk-dog and changed the customs of the People forever. They were now among the most respected of tribes on the plains. Since their alliance with the Head Splitters, their strength appeared invincible.

The medicine man was delighted that this intelligent young girl seemed interested in the traditions of the People. Perhaps she would choose to become a medicine woman. True, her branch of the family had produced more warriors, while the descendants of Owl had become medicine men, but this was not inflexible.

His own wife, Blue Dawn, was a valuable asset to his work, but none of their children seemed seriously to wish to follow in their steps. He badly needed an understudy, someone to whom he could pass the secrets of his art. There must be a custodian for the Elk-dog Medicine, the magic amulet handed down from Heads Off himself. It had originally been used in the mouth of the First Elk-dog, it was said, and contained the powerful medicine that allowed control of the animals. Its principle, that of the circle around the lower jaw, had been adapted to the use of a rawhide thong, the simply contrived "war bridle." The Spanish bit itself now had ceremonial significance, as the most powerful medicine of the People. The Southern band was called the Elk-dog band because of it.

There had been a short while, before Looks Far was born, when the bit had been stolen from his father, Horse Seeker. The search for and recovery of the amulet was one of the thrilling legends of the People.

Now, it was the duty of Looks Far to select the proper person to whom the Elk-dog Medicine would eventually be passed. As he watched the girl, Pale Star, growing and learning, he had begun to think that this might be the one.

She was interested and intelligent, thoughtful, and not inclined, even as a child, to act impulsively. Of course, if she chose to follow the warrior's path, like most of her family, so be it. It was her choice. Even if she chose to marry and seek her future in her own lodge as wife and mother, the decision belonged to her.

Meanwhile, Looks Far would answer the child's questions and encourage her in whatever she chose. For, like her mother, the medicine man felt that this child was special.

Her questions were sometimes frustrating. She was fascinated by the annual conflict between the Cold Maker from the northern mountains and the torch of Sun Boy. The People watched anxiously each winter as the symbolic struggle took place through the Moon of Long Nights and the Moon of Snows. There was always a feeling of relief when, in the Moon of Awakening, Sun Boy's new torch began to drive Cold Maker back, and the prairie awakened to the warm rays.

"But, Uncle, where does he get his new torch?"

"Who knows, little sister?" Looks Far would answer patiently. "From his lodge on the Other Side, I suppose."

Or, at the time of the burning of the grass, her questions again became frustrating. The girl knew, of course, that the grass must be burned in the Moon of Greening, so the buffalo would return.

"How do they know?"

"Know what, little one?"

"How do the buffalo know where to come?"

"Where it has been burned, of course."

"But how do they know where we have burned?"

"*Aiee*, I do not know. Their visions tell them."

"Do buffalo have visions?"

"All things have visions."

"Even rocks and trees? What sort of visions do rocks have?"

"How do I know what visions rocks have?"

He was almost irritable with her, and Pale Star sat quietly and hugged her knees against her chest. Her large dark eyes stared at him, still asking for the answer.

"Look, little one," he spoke more gently, "you ask questions which have no answers. When you are older, and go on your own vision quest, you may learn some of these things."

"It is good, Uncle."

The child jumped happily to her feet and skipped off toward her own lodge.

Looks Far watched her go, relighted his pipe with a twig from the fire, and settled against his willow backrest. He gave a long sigh.

"That one asks strange questions," observed Blue Dawn, busy at the cooking fire.

"*Aiee*," he smiled. "She makes me think. Do you know what sort of visions rocks and trees have?"

"No," his wife laughed, "I never wondered."

"But *she* wonders," the medicine man said thoughtfully. "Dawn, there is something special about this child. I feel strange things ahead for her."

"Good things, or bad?"

"Who knows?"

He was silent for a little while. He blew a cloud of fragrant blue smoke toward the hole at the apex of the lodge.

"Who knows? Perhaps both."

2
>> >> >>

The People scattered widely after the Sun Dance that year. The summer camps of the various bands were far-flung, even more so than usual.

The weather had turned hot and dry early in the season, even before the Moon of Roses was over. The buffalo returned, but not in large numbers. There were none of the usual great herds, darkening the prairie as far as eye could see. Something must be done at once. The available buffalo were scarcely enough to supply the People and their Head Splitter allies. Obviously, they must separate, moving far apart, to best utilize the thinly scattered herds.

There was discussion, of course, as to where the herds had gone. Some theorized that the buffalo had returned to the underworld, perhaps through the original opening made by the Old Man in the faraway past legendry of the People.

The older members of the tribe were divided as to why this had occurred. Some said it was merely the variation of the seasons. Some years were dry, some wet. This one was dry, and the buffalo searched for an area where the year was wetter.

A far grimmer interpretation suggested that the spirits were angry because of the alliance with the Head Splitters. There had been no year of such dryness before that alliance. Both tribes were being punished for the unnatural association, it was said.

"Do eagles mate with vultures?" was a common argument for those who espoused this theory.

The more thoughtful members of the People realized that neither tribe could have survived without the alliance. There was no point to the discussion.

Regardless of theories and reasons, it was necessary to disperse as quickly as possible at the end of the ceremonies. There was no casual stay to visit a few days with relatives and friends. The lodges were coming down by daylight of the first sun after the dance.

Each band sought the direction of its traditional summer hunting grounds. The Red Rocks, with perhaps the longest journey, were the first band to leave. One band of Head Splitters, pointing in the same direction, would accompany them for a few days. This, of course, set tongues to clucking in disapproval. There were dire predictions of further misfortune.

The Northern band, still not at full strength from a massacre by Blue Paints a generation ago, organized efficiently and moved onto the prairie, headed for their own area. The Mountain band moved Northwest at almost the same time.

The Southern, or Elk-dog, band of Pale Star's family was next in turn, their column pointing south and east. Their last glimpse of the site of the Sun Dance just finished showed the Eastern band milling about in uncertain, disorganized confusion. It was typical of that band, long known for its foolish ways.

"*Aiee*," someone observed, "the Eastern band will still be here when we return next year!"

Everyone laughed. There were jokes many generations old about the irrational behavior of this group. Despite their poor judgment, the Eastern band seemed to have a charmed existence, going happily on their way and emerging unscathed from dangerous situations that would have destroyed the more conventional bands.

Standing Bird, aging chief of the Elk-dog band, now led his people rapidly south. Several favorite camping areas were left behind, for sign of game was scarce. At one area, they paused, only to move on because the water supply seemed unreliable. Finally Standing Bird called for a day's rest and a council. Decisions must be made.

"My brothers," the chief began, after the ritual passing of the medicine pipe, "we have seen much thirst. Streams that we have never known to fail are dry. The grass is poor. We have seen no buffalo. What shall be done?"

There was silence for a moment, and a warrior rose to be recognized.

"My chief, what lies farther to the south? Who has been there?"

"I have, Black Wolf, in my youth," the old chief smiled, reminiscing. "There are hills, and many oaks, then more open plains beyond."

There were nods of approval, and a murmur ran through the circle. Standing Bird held up his hand for attention.

"But, my friends, there is less water and shorter grass than in our own country. At least, when I was there."

"What of the west?" asked another man.

"I can answer, my chief," volunteered another. "I grew up in the Red Rocks band. That, too, is a dry area at this season."

"It is no good to go back where we have been," someone observed.

"That leaves only the east," spoke the chief. "Has any of us been to that region?"

There was an excited buzz, then tense silence.

"My chief," someone asked, "is that not forest and hills?"

"So I have heard."

"Then there would be no buffalo?"

"Perhaps not. There must be deer. Looks Far, what say you?"

The medicine man rose thoughtfully.

"I do not know, my chief. We may need to try that way. There should be more water. I will cast the stones and ask a vision tonight, but I think we must go."

"Will we join the Eastern band?" spoke a young man from the rear.

There was a ripple of laughter, but the stern looks of the band chiefs said that it was no time for jokes.

"You may, if you wish," said Standing Bird sternly.

The circle became quiet.

"Now here is what we will do," the chief continued. "Three warriors will ride ahead to scout the country, and we will follow."

He paused and glanced at the medicine man.

"If, of course, Looks Far's medicine says it is good."

Looks Far nodded.

"I will ask, my chief."

Standing Bird clapped his hands to dismiss the council, and people scattered to the temporary campsites of their families.

For many sleeps the Elk-dog band moved to the east. They encountered occasional deer and once a bear, who caused a wide detour. To have to kill a bear would be very bad medicine, and to eat one almost equal to cannibalism.

Frustrated scouts returned to the main column from time to time, complaining that nothing could be seen. The forest grew heavier day by day and the small hills more numerous. Most of the time no one could see beyond the distance of a bow shot. It was very frustrating for the People, accustomed to far horizons. Everyone became more irritable, and quarrels were frequent.

At least they now encountered frequent streams. Finally, the chief called a halt.

"Here we will stay," he announced to the council. "If there is enough game, we can winter here and go home in the spring."

The People erected their lodges with some misgivings. There appeared to be enough grass to support the horses, in the sweeping meadow along the river. The hunt would be hard, though. The use of the bow, on foot in heavy timber, was far different than hunting buffalo on horseback.

"To hunt deer on foot," complained White Hawk. "*Aiee*, I have never had to feed my family this way!"

"It is all right," comforted Spotted Fawn, "it is only one season. The rains and the buffalo will be back next year."

As for Pale Star, it was a great adventure, exciting in its differences. There were new things to see and learn, new plants and small creatures that lived in the deep shadows of the woods. Fuel was easy to gather here, and she was intrigued by the opportunity.

Still, she found the heavy growth of trees everywhere to be oppressive. There was nowhere that she had found where one could see the horizon. Sun Boy crossed each evening to his lodge beyond earth's rim unseen, hidden behind the dark mass of a myriad of trees and brush.

Sounds of strange unseen night creatures made the girl's neck prickle with excitement as she lay in her robes in her parents' lodge. She was not afraid, exactly. It was actually a delicious thrill of excitement. Still, she would be glad when this stay was over, and the People could return to the Tallgrass Hills, where their medicine was strongest.

3

》》》

It was this longing for the open spaces, the desire to see the far horizons, that proved her undoing. Pale Star was gathering wood for the cooking fire, with her friend Painted Stick, and the other girl's brother, Chipmunk.

The three children had wandered a little way from the camp. The People had seen no other tribe since they came into the strange forested region, so they had become relaxed and perhaps careless. No one thought anything of it when the youngsters wandered farther into the woods to look for fuel. It was only reasonable, as the supply of dead sticks nearby was exhausted.

Still, no one had seen another human being from outside their own band. It was beginning to appear that their winter site was well chosen. They had encountered deer, and a few elk, and it seemed that their food supply for the season might be sufficient.

It was a golden sunlit day of late fall that the three children went gathering firewood. There was no urgency in their errand, and they paused to watch a flight of geese honking their way south. For a while they tossed pebbles and pinecones into the stream, and watched silvery minnows dart for safety.

A rabbit hopped across the glade and froze, motionless, while a red-tailed hawk circled to take another look. There had seemed to be motion there below, but now there was none. The hawk soared on and landed in a big dead tree at the top of the hill.

"Look," whispered Pale Star, "how the hawk sits to look from the tree. He must see far from so high a place."

"Can he see the whole world?" asked Chipmunk.

"Of course not, stupid one," scolded his sister. "No one can see the whole world."

"But wait," observed Pale Star. "He might see earth's rim. That can always be seen on the prairie, even when we move."

"Then where is it?" demanded Chipmunk.

"Beyond the trees, of course. Look, Chipmunk, if you could climb high enough, you could see over—"

Star paused, the sentence unfinished, as an idea struck her.

"Painted Stick! I think we can do it! Look, the tree where the hawk sits! There are limbs all the way up. We can climb and look!"

Before her friend could answer, Pale Star was running, bounding through the woods toward the tree.

"Star! Be careful," Painted Stick called, even while following after.

"Come on!" Star retorted.

She was already starting to climb when the others reached the base of the tree. The limbs were well spaced and easy to grasp near the trunk. There was only an occasional glistening bead of the old tree's sap to show that it had once been alive. These sugary deposits made climbing sticky but were not a hindrance to progress.

The hawk sounded a shrill cry of alarm high above and launched into the air. It circled and continued to scream at the intruder climbing toward its recently vacated perch.

Actually, Pale Star reached nowhere near the top. She paused and looked, over the tops of lesser trees below. In the pale haze of autumn, the forest stretched away as far as she could see, even to the west, where she knew her beloved prairie lay. Range after range of forested hills stretched into the far distance, becoming more blue and hazy until they were almost invisible against the blue and hazy sky. Still, she saw no open country.

"Can you see earth's rim?" Painted Stick called from below.

"Yes, but it is still covered with trees," Pale Star answered in disappointment. "I'm coming down."

The descent was more difficult than the climb. It was necessary to look carefully where she was preparing to place her foot with each step. Below her, Star could hear the other children, also having trouble with the retreat down the forest giant's long trunk. The hawk continued to circle and scream its outrage.

"Look out!" cried Chipmunk. "You are stepping on my hand!"

"Well, get out of the way," his sister retorted.

"Stop it!" called Pale Star, annoyed by the childish bickering as well as by her own frustrations. "Just go on down."

She reached for the next lower limb with her foot, feeling cautiously to test it under her weight. Below, out of sight through the tangle of dead limbs, Chipmunk was crying now. How irritating! Next time they would leave him behind.

There was a frightened little cry from Painted Stick and then, sudden silence. Even Chipmunk was no longer crying. Something was wrong.

"What is it?" she called. "Painted Stick? Are you there?"

An angry thought occurred to her. Had the two reached the ground and run to hide from her? It was the sort of childish prank that would occur to Painted

Stick. But that would not account for the little surprised exclamation from the other girl. No, something
was not as it should be.

Pale Star descended as rapidly as she could, pausing
to peer below when opportunity offered. The dead
limbs, so convenient to her upward climb, now re-
tarded her progress.

"Painted Stick? Chipmunk?" she called again. "Answer me!"

She was still half concerned and half angry, peering
through the lowest branches at the ground. Her concern changed instantly to terror.

A tall warrior held Painted Stick in a firm grasp, a
hand over her mouth, while another was in the process of tying her hands behind her. Chipmunk lay to
one side, already tied. Tears of frustration and fear
rolled down his plump cheeks and across the thong in
his mouth, which kept him from crying out.

Pale Star reached up to begin climbing again, but
paused to glance down at a sudden movement below.
Another man had moved around to an open space
where he could see her better and was preparing to
draw his bow.

"*Aho!*" someone called.

Pale Star looked over at the speaker, whose demean-
or suggested that he was a leader. He now, very
deliberately, began to address her in hand-sign talk.

"Come down or he will shoot you!"

She looked again at the man with the bow. It might
be possible to swing around the trunk before he loosed
an arrow, but it seemed unlikely.

"You cannot escape, girl. Come down," the leader
signed again.

It was true. She could stay in the tree only until she
became tired and lost her grip. The party of strangers
below could wait.

"We could burn your tree," suggested the man below.

The others laughed.

Pale Star was not deceived. They would not risk a

large blaze, which could attract the attention of her people.

Still, to descend and accept capture seemed the best course of action. The strangers had not harmed the other children yet. That was a good sign. They would be kept alive. Then there was the possibility of escape or rescue.

"I come down," she signaled clumsily with one hand.

The short distance to the ground was relatively easy, now. Star scrambled downward and dropped to the soft cushion of the forest floor. Men ran toward her.

"Stop!" she signed. "You will treat us properly! My father is a great warrior."

There was much laughter.

"Where?" one man signed in mock terror. "I am afraid!"

"I see no warrior," gestured the man who appeared to be the leader.

He reached for the girl. Star twisted away and sprinted for the bushes. Another warrior grabbed and missed, but one made a diving catch and his hand caught her ankle. She fell heavily, gasping for the breath that had been knocked from her lungs. Her captor sat on the wriggling girl, laughing, while others bound her arms behind her.

She started to scream, hoping against hope that some of her people would hear. The sound was choked off as someone forced a dirty rawhide thong between her teeth and pulled it tight behind her neck. She was jerked to her feet.

"Now," signaled the leader, "we go."

4

» » »

Star felt like a captive elk-dog as they followed single file along the forested path. The thong between her teeth cut painfully into the corners of her mouth, and she wondered whether the medicine knot around a horse's lower jaw was this uncomfortable.

Probably not, she decided. A horse could still open its mouth. She could not. It had taken only a few moments for her to discover that it was much easier to breathe if she did not try to struggle or cry out. Even to attempt opening her jaw produced more pressure against the already tender corners of her lips.

So she plodded on. It was not easy to keep her balance with her arms tied. Ahead of her was the broad back of a burly warrior, and she could hear the tread of another close behind her. She caught an occasional glimpse of Chipmunk, tied as she was and stumbling along in the column ahead. Painted Stick was somewhere behind.

In Star's thoughts was the idea that the People would look for them, would follow and rescue. She must leave a trail. There were excellent trackers among the People, but she must help in any way possible.

She staggered from side to side, appearing weaker than she actually felt. That would be good strategy, anyway. But her main purpose was to leave signs that could be read by the trackers. She kicked a pile of pine needles, scattering them across the path, apparently by accident. Again, her foot crushed a clump of ferns beside the trail.

It was not until the girl blatantly left a moccasined footprint in a muddy spot that her captors seemed to notice. She was jerked roughly to a halt by the thongs on her arms, while the man behind her called out to the others.

They gathered around while he pointed to the footprint. Their leader confronted her.

"You will not leave sign!" he gestured angrily. "We will kill you!"

Star tried to appear terrified, and shook her head emphatically, but she was pleased. Her captors *were* afraid of pursuit. She did not especially fear the threat of death. If that had been the aim of this party, they would have killed the captives immediately. Instead, they were going to great lengths to keep them alive.

Of course, the girl had some misgivings as to the reasons for this action on the part of her captors. *Why* were they to be kept alive? That answer, she was certain, would be found eventually. Meanwhile, as long as they were alive, there was the possibility of escape or rescue. If they were dead, the game was over.

So she would be more cautious with her leaving of a trail for the trackers.

She watched while one of the warriors, stepping cautiously, brought a flat rock and placed it on her footprint. The men nodded, with grunts of approval, and the march resumed.

There were seven of them. Star had attempted to gather as much information as she could. These were of a tribe unknown to the People. At least to Pale Star.

They carried short bows, knives at their waists, but she saw no axes or war clubs. And, she now realized, none carried spears or lances.

She attempted to analyze these observations. It was logical, she supposed, that hunters in the woods did not need spears. She remembered her father's complaint about the different mode of hunting. Without horses to hunt running buffalo, a lance was of little use.

She was more puzzled by the absence of hand weapons. Would not a war party, such as this appeared to be, need axes or war clubs? It was some time before she realized that a weapon which must swing in an arc might be limited by the obstruction of trees and brush. These people of the forest had reasons of their own for their tools and weapons. Star was already thinking of them as the Forest People.

Their garments were of unfamiliar pattern, of course, as well as the style of their hair. The design of the ornamentation on their shirts and leggings was strange, too, far from the geometric symmetry of those of the People.

Their moccasins were of completely different style from any she had seen. More strange than those of the Growers, even. Growers lived in villages along the streams and traded their produce to the hunting tribes for meat and skins. Star had always thought it strange that people would live as the Growers did, in half-buried lodges. Now she could scarcely imagine what sort of customs these Forest People might practice.

The party stopped for a brief rest near a spring that came from the hillside. The warriors knelt and scooped water with their palms, sucking noisily. No one seemed to think of the prisoners.

Pale Star managed to attract the attention of the leader and motioned to the water with her head and eyes. The man smiled, spoke something to the others, and rose to loosen the thong in her mouth. Someone did the same for the others.

Chipmunk began to cry.

"Be still, Chipmunk," Star hissed at him. "You are a man of the People. Where is your pride?"

She stood erect, facing the leader, trying to call attention to her tied hands.

"My chief," she spoke formally, in her own tongue, smiling her friendliest smile, "your mother eats dung. I know your Forest People are stupid, but is there one among you who can see that we cannot drink while our hands are tied?"

There was a gasp from Painted Stick.

"Do not talk so, Star," she whimpered. "They will kill us."

"No, if they wished to, they would have already. Besides, they do not know our tongue. If we smile, they will think anything we say is good."

The other girl giggled nervously, and Chipmunk sniffed quietly, still not convinced.

Star faced her captors again, motioning to her bound hands and to the water. The chief nodded.

"You will not run away," he gestured in sign-talk.

It was a statement, not a question. Pale Star thought for a moment. She could not escape without her companions. They must stay together to help each other, for the present, at least.

She nodded agreement. The chief released her bonds, and she stood rubbing her wrists for a moment.

"The others, also," she signed. "They will not run."

The man looked questioningly at the other children.

"Do not try to run," Star called.

Both shook their heads. The tall chief nodded, and a couple of the warriors loosened their bonds also. Chipmunk started eagerly toward the water.

"Remember your pride, Chipmunk," Star called.

The boy slowed and approached the spring with some degree of dignity. Star turned again to the leader.

"Thank you, my chief," she signed. "We can travel better now. Where are we going?"

Star's mind was racing. If she could establish communication with these people, she could learn more of their ways. This would make escape easier. The appearance of cooperation would also cause them to relax their attention to the captives.

The leader, however, seemed to understand completely what she was attempting. He chuckled sarcastically.

"You will see," he gestured. "Now drink, before you are tied again."

There was no questioning the authority in his manner. Pale Star drank.

5

» » »

S tar did manage to accomplish one victory during this stop. She was able to convince the leader that they could travel better with hands tied in front. It was a small thing, but true, and much more comfortable.

No mention was made of the mouth gags, for which the children were grateful. Apparently their captors no longer considered their silence necessary. They must consider that they were now in their own territory. Star had not given up the idea of pursuit and rescue, however.

They traveled rapidly throughout the day. Their progress was difficult for the girl to evaluate. She was accustomed to travel on the open, rolling plains, the slowly changing shapes of distant grassy hills and the darker stripes of the wooded watercourses. Here there was the oppressive sameness of heavy forests.

When they did occasionally come to a clearing or hilltop, there was nothing to see but more trees. She felt at times that the dark forest was closing in on her. It was almost the feeling she had had once in a Grower village.

She had gone with her mother to trade and had peered curiously into one of the mud-and-brush lodges. It was dark, forbidding, and poorly ventilated. It smelled heavily of body scent, almost like a bear's den. Star had quickly withdrawn in alarm. She did not understand how people could live like that, without the clean sweep of the wind around the lodges.

One thing the girl did manage to observe as they traveled. They were moving in a generally eastern direction. Again it was difficult to tell; the trail had so many twists and turns. She observed that the sun was usually shining from her right on the longer straight portions of the path. The shadows of the trees fell across open spaces from right to left. So, with Sun Boy making his daily run across the southern sky, they must be traveling east.

Her impression was reinforced as the shadows lengthened. By evening, the rays of Sun Boy's torch were coming from almost directly behind her. There was a great sense of satisfaction that she had been able to maintain her sense of position.

They stopped for the night, and the warriors built small fires for warmth. Star requested with gestures that their hands be untied. The leader seemed to consider for a long time but finally nodded.

"You will not run away," he signed. "There are many bears in the woods."

A couple of the warriors chuckled, and she knew the chief was lying. His suggestion would be effective, however. With this idea firmly in their minds, there was no possibility that the other children could be persuaded to escape into the darkness. Anyway, rescue would probably come tonight.

She wondered whether these Forest People fought at night. The Head Splitters feared to die in darkness, lest their spirits not find the way to the Other World. The People had no such taboo and had used this difference against the Head Splitters long ago. When they became allies, joining against a common invader, their differences were used to good advantage. The

Head Splitters attacked by day, the People at night, keeping the enemy exhausted, confused, and irritated.

Now, Pale Star wondered what customs of her captors could be used against them. She approached the chief conversationally.

"How are you called, my chief?" she signed.

The man glanced at her, irritated for a moment. Then he relented.

"I am White Bear."

"I am called Pale Star. My father is White Hawk, a chief of the People."

There was a moment of confusion. Each tribe's name for itself usually meant "the people," so the hand-sign was similar. White Bear looked sharply at her, then shrugged.

"That is of no concern to me, girl."

It was very tempting to angrily threaten, but it would be of little use. She would do better to maintain good communications. She spread her hands in helpless question.

"What do you wish with us?"

He did not answer her question but handed her a few strips of dried meat.

"Go and eat. Give to the others. You must rest, travel far tomorrow."

Star nodded as cheerfully as she could and took the food to the others.

"Here, eat. We must keep our strength."

They chewed the leathery strips of venison. It was stronger in flavor than the buffalo of their own country, but acceptable to hungry young appetites.

"Do you think our people will come for us?" Painted Stick asked.

"Of course," Star replied confidently.

She was not as sure as she sounded.

"But," she continued, "we must keep ourselves in good shape. We may have to help or to escape and join them when they come."

"What will these people do with us? If our warriors do not come, I mean?" Painted Stick wondered.

"I do not know," snapped Star irritably. "We will find out."

"They will eat us!" whimpered Chipmunk.

"Stop that," Star scolded. "People do not eat people."

"Some do," the other girl offered. "I have heard."

Star had heard, too, of tribes far to the south who were said to eat their enemies' hearts. But they must not give way to panic.

"That is not true," she insisted. "And, if it is, not here."

"But—"

"Be still, Painted Stick! We have enough to worry about!"

Star only caught a glimpse of a startled look in the eyes of her friend before something struck her from behind. She rolled on the ground, head ringing from the blow she had received. A warrior stood over her, ready to cuff her again.

"You talk much," he signed. "Be quiet, now."

White Bear hurried forward and a mild argument ensued. Pale Star got the impression that the chief was protesting such treatment. Not from sympathy or pity, she was sure, but from a wish to maintain the prisoners in good condition.

The chief snapped a few words, and men moved forward to separate the prisoners for the night. Pale Star, it appeared, would stay with the chief, the others with two other men. It began to appear that the captives were the exclusive property of these individuals.

White Bear knotted a thong around her ankle and the other end to his own. There was perhaps an arm's length between. She saw that the other prisoners were being similarly fettered. That would make escape more difficult, but not impossible.

She rolled in the ragged scrap of a robe that he tossed her, with legs drawn up in fetal position. Her body would lose less warmth in this posture. If necessary, she could snuggle close to her captor for warmth, but she would prefer not to.

There was another advantage to the posture she

assumed. She could reach her ankles and work with her fingers on the rawhide knots. She would think of something. Several possibilities had opened up for her, though they were still vague and unformed.

The most important event of the evening, perhaps, was the thong. In the minor flurry of excitement after she was knocked to the ground, Star had noticed a slender piece of rawhide that someone had dropped. She contrived to stumble and fall before anyone noticed its loss. To observers in the twilight, she appeared only to brush debris from her dress and adjust it after her fall.

Yet, when she rose and obediently followed White Bear, the thong rested inside her garment. She did not yet know how it could be used, but she was certain it would be useful.

There was little sleep for Pale Star that night. She expected an attack by the rescue party at any time. There was no way she could know that the rescue would not come. Unfamiliar with the strange country, they had mistaken which direction the children had taken from camp. The trackers had followed the wrong trail, winding through dense woods and hills.

White Hawk and the rescue party camped for the night, tired, anxious, and completely frustrated. They had finally realized they were on the wrong trail, but there was little they could do now.

They were nearly a day's travel from where the captives spent a restless night. Meanwhile, the signs needed by the trackers were being destroyed by the wind, the passage of time, and the wild creatures of the woods. The trail was growing cold.

6

≫ ≫ ≫

It was a cold, uncomfortable night. Each time Star dozed off or inadvertently moved the leg to which her fetter was attached, White Bear wakened. Once he cuffed her irritably.

She realized that if she moved somewhat closer to her captor, there was more slack in the thong. It was a cautious trade-off. She did not wish to be any nearer than was necessary, but she felt she must. By extending her tied leg toward the man, she was able to relax and rest a little.

It was disappointing, as the party rose with the sun, to realize that the rescue party had not come. Perhaps they had simply not overtaken the rapidly traveling Forest People yet. But in her heart Pale Star knew the truth. Something had gone wrong. The rescue party had been unable to find the trail or had been prevented from doing so. An uneasy thought flashed through her head that the camp of the People had been attacked, perhaps everyone killed.

She immediately rejected that possibility. If it were true, their captors would know of it. They would be arrogant and boastful. Instead, they were behaving in a secretive manner, moving rapidly away from the scene of the abduction. Star began to think that this had been merely a chance encounter, one in which a hunting party had taken advantage of the opportunity to seize the children.

The stealing of children was not uncommon. Before the alliance with the Head Splitters, that custom had been the major point of friction between them and the People. Head Splitters had loved to abduct girls and young women of the People for wives. "Our women are prettier than theirs," the People had said for many generations.

There was some accuracy in this oft-repeated truism. Women of the People were traditionally tall, long-legged, with willowy grace and fine features.

Pale Star wondered if it was a factor in this abduction. She looked down critically at her body. It was probable that she would be tall when she was fully grown. She had grown nearly a hand's span in the past season, and there was much height in her family. True, her breasts had just begun to swell, and the sensitive nipples barely caused a bulge inside her soft buckskin dress.

She realized that to her abductors, her womanhood might be part of her worth. She knew that the captives were being kept alive because of their value. Originally, she had wondered if they might be held for ransom. Now, it seemed unlikely. The Forest people were traveling *away* from the area where the People were camped, as rapidly as was practical.

This brought one thought to her mind again, that of rescue. She continued to try to leave trail sign, but she had already decided that it was useless. With so great a head start, there was little chance that the men of her band could overtake the retreating abductors. Whatever happened from this morning on, she was now on her own.

At the next stop, Star tried to evaluate how the other captives were faring. Chipmunk seemed to have overcome his original terror. His captor was attempting to communicate with the boy, giving him bites of dried meat and teasing him in a friendly way. Chipmunk was chuckling over the warrior's exaggerated antics. Apparently the boy's hands had not even been tied on the trail.

"Chipmunk, it is good to have friends," Star called, "but remember you are of the People."

Painted Stick seemed to be doing well. Her temperament was that of one who never becomes very excited under any circumstances. She would adapt. Pale Star smiled at the other girl across the clearing and waved to her. Her friend returned the wave.

Star turned to attempt conversation with White Bear, in sign talk.

"Is yours a hunting party?"

The chief only glanced at her in mild annoyance.

"How many sleeps until we reach your lodge?"

She realized that she had no knowledge of these people at all, and did not even know what their lodges might be. Permanent dwellings like those of the Growers, probably, made of trees and mud. She wondered if she could stand the confinement of such a place. She hoped that her questions about the lodge of her captor might give her more information. White Bear seemed intent on discouraging her inquiry, however.

"Silence!" he gestured. "You rest now."

It was almost at that moment that a shout was heard in the woods. Men jumped on their feet, grabbing weapons as they ran.

For a moment, Star believed that a rescue party had overtaken the travelers. Then she realized that such hopes were groundless. Rescuers would not shout to indicate their presence. Besides, the hail, which seemed to announce a friendly contact, came from the north, not from the west from where they had come.

The rest stop was at a large, clear spring, and there were paths or trails from several directions, probably used by people and animals for generations. It was probably a well-known meeting place and campsite for travelers in the area.

The call had come from one of the well-beaten trails, and all eyes now turned in that direction. Now that the initial surprise had passed, the warriors began to relax. They realized, as Star had done, that an enemy does not announce himself.

They had not long to wait. A man emerged from the trees, right hand raised, palm outward, in peaceful salute. He carried a large pack on his shoulders, and a woman walked behind him with a similar burden.

The two did not pause but moved straight to the spring, where they shrugged their packs to the ground. The man's eyes swept quickly around the clearing.

"Greetings, my brothers," he signed carelessly before kneeling to drink.

The others simply stood and waited, while the couple drank long and eagerly. Theirs must have been a mighty thirst.

Star watched the newcomers with care. She must be aware of any possible assistance in escape, even if only by distraction. They appeared to be of a tribe other than that of her captors. The man's hair was of a different style, with long braids rather than the odd closely cropped manner of White Bear and the others. His garments, too, were constructed differently. The girl received the impression that here were two tribes known to each other, perhaps even allies. This idea became more prominent as the stranger rose, wiped his mouth on his sleeve, and sighed deeply.

"That is good," he gestured in sign-talk. "It is very dry to the north."

There were noncommittal nods of understanding and agreement, then another wait for the stranger to make himself known.

Star watched with great interest. If this proceeded in sign-talk, she would be able to follow the conversation. There would be certain customs to observe, probably similar to those of her own people. The newcomer would introduce himself to the chief, pay his respects,

and explain his mission in the other's country. Her
impressions soon proved correct.

"Which is your chief?" the stranger asked.

Several indicated White Bear, who now stepped
forward.

"I am White Bear, chief of the people," he indicated,
again confusing Star for a moment by his use of the
sign for "people" or "humans." "How are you called?"

"I have been called many things," the newcomer
replied. "Just now I am called a traveler."

"Where are your people?"

"Far to the north, my chief. My wife, here, is of
your country. We come to winter with her people."

As the conversation progressed, Star gathered that
the woman was from a tribe closely allied to the
Forest people, but separate. The husband, who whimsi-
cally called himself Traveler, was from a tribe quite
distant.

He opened his pack to produce a pouch of tobacco
and presented a pipeful to White Bear. It was the
signal for a semiformal "smoke," and the group settled to smoke and visit for a time.

Star was impatient. It occurred to her that she might
run, since she was still untied from being released to
drink. She quickly saw that it was a poor idea and
relaxed to learn what she could.

The home village of this, a hunting party, White
Bear related, was still some three sleeps away. They
had encountered signs of intruders from the plains,
and in the process of scouting had captured the three
children.

"What will you do with them?" Traveler asked.

"Who knows?" White Bear shrugged. "Sell them,
maybe."

Traveler nodded understandingly.

"They look strong. A little thin, perhaps."

"You wish them?"

"No, my chief," the newcomer smiled. "I have no
wish for burdens of this sort."

Through the rest of the day, Star watched Traveler and his wife. The couple had elected to join the party of White Bear for the present, since their direction of travel was basically the same.

The warriors of the Forest people seemed fascinated by this chance to listen to stories from a far tribe. The woman spoke some of their tongue, and with this and sign talk communication proved easy. It was resumed at each rest stop. Their captors were so distracted that no one seemed to notice that the hands of the children were not retied.

Star began to see possibilities for escape. Whenever a chance offered, she began to tell the others of her plan. It would require alert action, all at one time, with no mistakes. Tonight seemed their best opportunity, while the warriors of White Bear were still absorbed in the stories of Traveler.

At their camp that evening, Star completed her plans.

"We will meet at the rocky hill we passed a while ago," she told the others, "but you must be ready.

When I call out, like *kookooskoos* the owl, we will slip away."

"But we will be tied, Star," Chipmunk whined.

"Of course. You must untie your foot and be ready."

"They will catch us."

"Maybe so, but we will try."

"I don't know, Star," the boy whimpered. "What if we can't untie the thong?"

"Then we will leave you," snapped his sister. "Chipmunk, you be ready, because we are going."

For a long time after their captors retired, Star watched the Seven Hunters circle the Real-star. They must wait until the warriors relaxed, the fire burned low, and most of the camp was asleep.

It had been both an advantage and an irritation that Traveler and his wife were present. The man and his stories provided a very useful distraction. However, Star had mixed feelings. The entertainment caused everyone to stay up later, to keep the fire built up, and to continue the amusing evening.

Finally, when it seemed nearly morning, the camp was quiet and the light from the fire had died. Star listened to the regular breathing of White Bear for a while and then carefully began to pick at the knots on her ankle.

Once she stopped in terror as the big man stirred and mumbled in his sleep. He turned on his back and flung an arm which landed across her face and head. Star was ready, and managed to irritably push the arm away with an apparently sleepy protest. Her captor mumbled and turned his back to her, barely breaking the regular rhythm of his breathing. She turned again to the knotted thong.

Slowly, the girl loosened the knots, carefully untied the rawhide fetters, and lay waiting. She must allow the others plenty of time. Chipmunk, especially, was not as adept as the older girls. He would require more time to loosen his bonds. Star lay, impatient, trying to gauge how long she should allow.

It was during this time of waiting that an idea came to her. She smiled to herself and slipped a hand inside her dress to bring out the thong she secretly carried. Very quietly she reached over and tied one end to a stout sapling. Then she unrolled the thong to its full length. Yes, it would reach nicely, with some to spare.

She began to knot the free end of her thong to the one on White Bear's leg. She thought with amusement that she would like to watch when he arose.

Now it was finished. She had only to slip away, locate any sentries, and withdraw to the woods a little way to give the signal. She was almost ready to rise to hands and knees to crawl into the darkness when a movement overhead caught the corner of her eye. She looked quickly, in time to see a silent dark shape glide across the clearing, blotting out a handful of stars as it passed.

The owl moved noiselessly on fixed wings toward a dead stub at the edge of the woods. At the last moment the soft wings changed their position, and the bird swept upward in a graceful curve to land on the dead trunk. She could see the outline of the owl's head and ears as it peered down into the clearing. Some slight motion on the part of a fur-covered sleeper might have caught the attention of the great hunting bird. Now it would sit and watch, to see if the movement's source might be a potential meal.

Star held her breath. The thing she feared now was that *kookooskoos* would give his hunting call, which was also their signal. The other children would mistake this for her signal cry or else see the owl and ignore the signal when she did give it. *Aiee*, this was not going well.

She saw the bird cock its head to one side and the other, and then stretch stiffly upward to call out. Fascinated, she heard the hollow rendition of the owl's name boom through the night. It was louder than she had expected.

She had expected to give the call herself, quietly

and from some distance away. Now she was undecided whether to jump up and run into the darkness
or to remain still.

"*Kookooskoos!*" came the owl's deep cry again.

Around the clearing, men were stirring, disturbed
from sleep, mumbling irritably.

Now Star had another cause for concern. If the others were untied, or partly so, and their captors were
awakening, the escape attempt would be discovered.
For a moment she considered trying to retie her own
leg, but she knew there was no time.

Her thoughts were cut short by a yell of alarm from
Chipmunk. Someone had tossed dry fuel on one of the
fires and it now blazed up, flooding the area with
light.

Chipmunk was struggling with his captor, who held
the boy by one arm and jerked him roughly back
toward the others. The plan had gone wrong, the real
owl mistaken for the signal. The culprit, alarmed,
now spread silent wings and glided away in the night.

Star still stood, undecided whether to run or stay
and be recaptured. Too late, she decided to run.

White Bear lurched to his feet and darted after her.
She slipped away, eluding his grasp. She was aware of
a grunt of surprise and glanced back in time to see the
chief yanked from his feet by the thong around his
ankle. He fell heavily, landing partly in the coals of
his campfire and rolling aside with a roar of pain and
rage.

The girl paused just a moment too long. As she
turned to run again, she was grasped firmly from behind, arms pinned to her sides. She heard the man
who held her laughing. She tried to bite him but could
not reach him with her teeth.

Furious, she stopped struggling. It would do no good
now.

White Bear came over, the front of his buckskin
shirt scorched and blackened across one shoulder. He
carried the thongs she had so carefully knotted.

Roughly, he jerked her hands behind her and tied them cruelly tight. Then he shoved her to the ground.

Star rolled to break the fall, and saw White Bear grudgingly give the thank sign to Traveler, who had stopped her escape.

The outsider seemed to be doing his best to refrain from laughing.

8
>> >> >>

Pale Star watched the conversation, carried on in sign talk, in fascinated disbelief. White Bear and Traveler were bargaining, arguing over a trade. The bickering had begun at daylight.

No one had slept well after the abortive escape try. The camp was restless, and finally men began to rise and prepare for the day's journey. It was at this point that Traveler approached the group's leader.

"This one gives you trouble," he signed, indicating Star. "Trade her to me and be rid of her."

"Why do you want her?" asked the chief suspiciously. "I have no wish to trade."

"The girl is not worth much," Traveler agreed, "but I like her spirit. I might find some small thing to trade."

"She is worth much," signed the other indignantly. "You have nothing that I want, but what would you offer?"

Star understood the scene completely. Many times she had watched the same sparring and maneuvering over a horse trade. Sometimes it had even been, like this scene, carried on in sign-talk. Her own tribe and their allies, the Head Splitters, loved to race and trade horses. It gave her a strange, panicky feeling to realize that this time she was the horse they would bargain for.

"I have things in my pack," Traveler gestured indifferently.

"I will look. You wish all three?"

"No, no. Only this scrawny one. I could not afford the better ones."

Star was instantly furious, with a strange mixture of pride and resentment. Despite her fear and apprehension at being traded like a horse, she would have preferred that the prospective buyer hold a little more regard for her worth.

"She is strong!" boasted White Bear. "Here, feel her strength."

He felt her arms and legs, and invited the other to do so.

"She can work hard," he continued. "Besides, she will soon be a woman. She is pretty, yes? She will make a man's bed warm in the winter. Maybe I will keep her."

"This is only a child," scoffed Traveler.

He pinched her arms, legs, and buttocks gently, and ran his hands over her small breasts.

"Ah, no, there is not enough meat here to warm a bed. But I will offer some small things anyway."

The girl burned with embarrassment. How demeaning, this forced role as the major object in a horse trade. You will see, she vowed to herself, either one of you. Your bed might be dangerous. She remembered the story of her grandmother. As a young warrior woman, Running Eagle had killed a war chief who held her captive. Yes, in his own bed.

Of course she realized the reasons for the present stage of bargaining. The potential buyer was attempting to make her appear worth less in the trade, while the seller tried to overstate her value. Star was slightly

confused as to whether she would prefer to be worth
more or less at this point.

Over all was the shame and embarrassment of being
handled, prodded, and poked like a horse in a trade.
She knew that some tribes held women in poor regard, but it had never quite impressed her fully. Among
the People, women were highly regarded. She could
not imagine a scene such as this over a captive in her
own tribe.

"Well, let us look anyway," White Bear spread his
hands in a nonchalant shrug.

Traveler opened the thongs of his pack and began to
draw out small items of value. First he spread a small
skin between the two scated men and placed a stone
knife and a couple of arrow points on it. Other men
began to drift over to watch.

"These things for the girl."

White Bear's answer was an indignant wave of the
hand. It was customary, of course, to ridicule the first
offer. Traveler cheerfully picked up the implements
and tried again.

This time it was a knife of fine quality, the shiny
black stone from far away that one rarely sees.

"This stone is made in the fires below the earth,"
Traveler indicated importantly.

White Bear picked up the volcanic obsidian blade
and tested its edge with his thumb, trying not to
appear too interested. Finally he tossed the knife back
on the skin.

"I have a knife," he pointed to the sheath at his
waist. "You have nothing else?"

There was the suggestion of a murmur around the
circle. White Bear had turned down an offer of great
value. The black knife was of the best material and
workmanship. He was driving a hard trade.

Traveler spread his hands in question as if bewildered by the refusal.

"I have a medicine pipe," he offered.

"Let me see it."

Traveler drew forth a long quill-decorated bag with

fluttering buckskin fringes. It was a thing of great beauty. He held it out toward White Bear, who took it carefully and pulled the pipe out of the case.

There was a short, terse remark from Traveler's wife, but he waved her aside.

"This red medicine stone comes only from one place, my chief, a sacred place far to the north."

White Bear looked at him for a moment in stony silence.

"Of course," he signaled. "Do you think I have never seen a medicine pipe?"

All the watchers, even Star herself, stood aghast as the chief returned the pipe to its case and handed it back.

"No," he signed, starting to rise.

Traveler was perhaps more surprised than anyone. He had apparently expected the pipe to carry the trade.

"Wait, my chief," he gestured, confused. "I have nothing else. What do you wish?"

White Bear was standing now.

"Your knife," he pointed to the other man's waist.

Somewhere in the past day, White Bear had seen that there was something special about Traveler's belt knife. He also realized, after the round of bargaining, that the other man wanted the girl badly enough to give almost anything he owned.

"My knife? I could not give this up!"

"So be it!"

White Bear turned away.

Traveler slid the weapon from its sheath and looked at it long and hard.

Star stifled a gasp. She had not noticed it before. Possibly he had not even unsheathed it. The knife was long and slender, tapering to a sharp tip. Its handle was smooth and round and it appeared well balanced.

The thing which caught the girl's attention, however, was the material from which the knife was made. The substance was, in appearance and color, exactly like that of the Elk-dog Medicine of the People, the Spanish bit. It was shiny and smooth, with the cutting edge straight rather than uneven, as were all the knives she had ever seen. From where she stood, Star was certain that this was a special knife.

There was a gasp around the circle. Apparently no one else had seen the knife either.

"Wait—" Traveler seemed indecisive. "For all three?"

White Bear turned back indignantly.

"Of course not! This is the one you want."

It appeared that Traveler, a trader by vocation, had been outtraded.

"It is good," he nodded, handing the knife to the chief.

His wife began a high-pitched harangue, apparently accusing Traveler of all manner of idiocy, until he spoke sharply to her. Then she subsided, and the others chuckled as they prepared to travel.

"Come on, girl," motioned Traveler. "I hope you are worth it."

He seemed not entirely pleased with his bargain.

Star's head was still reeling. The fact that she now had a different captor had not really reached her consciousness yet. Besides, her present status, which she considered temporary anyway, was insignificant compared to what she had just seen.

It was known among her people that the Elk-dog Medicine of her ancestor, Heads Off, was very powerful. It was supposed that part of its strength came from the strange substance from which it was made. Hard, smooth, and heavy, it could be warm or cool to the touch. Looks Far had allowed her to hold it for a moment once.

Now, she had seen a knife made of the same material. She longed to know more about it. Where had it come from, and how had Traveler acquired it?

9

» » »

Pale Star's shock at being bargained over and sold like a horse was almost overshadowed by the incident of the medicine knife. It was apparent that Traveler had had no intention of giving up the knife. Perhaps, even, he had not even wanted the others to know of it.

Somehow, White Bear had learned of it, perhaps accidently. He was also aware of Traveler's strong wish to own the captive. He had manipulated the situation to outwit and outtrade the trader.

Now White Bear, glorying in his triumph, was showing the knife to his warriors, arrogantly using it for minor tasks just for the opportunity to gloat. Once he unsheathed the medicine knife only to cut a strip of dried meat, which he could easily have broken or bitten in two.

Star resented, somehow, his vulgar display. It was too important a medicine object, she felt, to use in this way. However, it gave her more of an opportunity to see it.

She marveled at the smooth polish of the blade, at

the way a reflected ray of sunlight sparkled from its surface. It reminded her of the silvery flash of minnows in a sunlit stream. The knife's edge appeared extremely sharp. She could imagine, as White Bear held and turned the implement for all to see, that blue fire licked along its edge.

The girl was not certain why she was so attracted to the knife. Perhaps the affinity had to do with her own heritage, she thought. The more glimpses she had of the thing, the more certain she became that it was of the same substance as her tribe's Elk-dog Medicine. Who could question its power?

In her mind's eye, she began to fantasize as they walked that morning. When the time was right, she would not only escape but steal the medicine knife as well. Then she and the other children would return to the People. She would be recognized, though young, as a woman with strong medicine. It was a very attractive picture. She must watch for the opportunity to carry it out.

At a rest stop, she confided the outline of her plan to her fellow captives.

"So you must be ready when I say," Star finished.

"But, Star," protested Painted Stick, "we could not escape before. This would be even harder."

"I know, but that was the fault of *kookooskoos.* Next time we will plan better, and there will be no mistakes. I will let you know."

Men were rising and shouldering their packs now. Traveler came over and grasped Star's arm, gently but firmly. He drew out a thong and knotted it around the wrist.

"What is this?" she protested in sign-talk. "You have not tied me before!"

"Be still."

Traveler tied the other end of the long cord to his own waist. Then he turned to White Bear and began to sign.

"Here we part, my chief. My wife's people live that way."

Traveler pointed to one of the paths through the woods. This was another of the stopping places with paths going in various directions.

Quickly, Star noted that Traveler had indicated south. Now he gave a tug on her fetter as he shouldered his pack. His wife had already stepped toward the wooded path.

It was all happening too rapidly. She wished to talk to the other children.

"You walk ahead," Traveler signed to her.

Star looked back. Chipmunk and Painted Stick were staring with astonishment, not quite comprehending what was happening.

"Star!" cried the other girl, on the verge of tears.

"Keep your pride," called Pale Star. "Remember we are of the People. Do not let them see weakness! Watch for your chance to escape and go home. Watch the direction they take. Keep the—"

She was interrupted by a shove from Traveler and stumbled forward after his wife. Anger burned for a moment, and she turned on her captor.

"Do not push me," she signed. "I can walk without help."

"Then do it!"

She turned and strode forward, still burning with anger. In the space of a few heartbeats the woods had closed around them and the other party was gone.

Star moved on, keeping the woman ahead within sight. She had little trouble keeping up, her long legs accustomed to the distances of far horizons. Occasionally, in fact, she drew a step or two ahead of Traveler, and there was an annoying tug on her left wrist.

Some time later, when they stopped for a brief rest, Star asked that the thong be removed.

"I can walk faster," she pointed out.

The older woman unleashed a tirade of words in her own tongue. She was apparently not happy at all over her husband's trade. Finally Traveler silenced her with a wave of his hand.

"You will promise not to run away?" he asked Star in sign talk.

She was silent a moment.

"I cannot promise that, my chief. I am of the People. I will escape when I can."

Traveler threw up his hands in dismay.

"Listen, little one. You are in strange country, and winter is near. Give your promise for now."

"I can change it later?"

"It is good. You will let me know when?"

She nodded agreement and held out her wrist. Traveler cut the thong. His wife again started her torrent of invective, but again he stopped her. He spoke a few words, then turned back to the girl.

"I have told Plum Leaf that you and I have a bargain. You will not run unless you first tell me the agreement is finished. Agreed?"

Star nodded, fully aware of the black looks from Plum Leaf.

"One more thing. If you break your bargain, Plum Leaf says she will kill you."

Star turned to the woman.

"If I am dead, I am of no use to you. I could not even be sold. Still, a woman of my tribe keeps her promises. I agree to the bargain."

Traveler chuckled, the first time Star had heard him do so since his trade with White Bear.

"It is good," he signed. "Girl, I like your spirit. Tell me, how are you called?"

"I am Pale Star."

Traveler nodded.

"We will call you so. Yet, I am made to believe that this Star is not a pale one."

He chuckled again at his little joke.

"But come, let us go on. Cold Maker comes soon."

In this way, the three established an uneasy truce. Star was satisfied. Her agreement would give her more freedom, and when she wished, she could end it. She had only to say so.

10

» » »

Cold Maker did come soon. It was the following day that a cold wind began to rattle through the woods behind them, sending a chill through their bones. Sun Boy did not rise at all, and the sky remained gray and overcast. It was a big change from the warmth of the lazy autumn.

Traveler and Plum Leaf kept casting anxious glances at the sky. Star was anxious, too. She was not familiar with the climate here, but the dark sky was foreboding. Among her own people, this day would be a sign to finish preparing for winter. They would be checking their piles of firewood, stuffing dry grass into the space behind the lodge lining, and erecting brush windbreaks. It was certainly no time to be traveling.

Finally, to Star's great relief, Traveler called a halt. The girl estimated that it must be a little past the height of Sun Boy's run, though he was not seen.

Traveler pointed to a spot against an abrupt south slope, well sheltered from the northwest wind and screened by thick bushes. Plum Leaf motioned to the girl and dropped her pack on a level spot.

Star was completely baffled. They should be erecting a lodge of some sort, but what sort?

"What do you wish?" she signed, puzzled.

"We build a lodge, stupid one," answered Plum Leaf.

"Of what?"

"Brush, of course."

Again, Star did not understand. The People used
brush shelters, but only in summer, and those had
open sides.

"You gather firewood," Traveler signed. "We will
build the lodge."

The gathering of fuel was a thing she understood.
Another time she would understand the brush lodge.
She had a tendency to scorn the whole idea and remained a little uneasy about it. Would a tribe so
primitive that they built brush lodges really understand how to prepare for winter? She longed for the
safety and comfort of her father's lodge, highly developed and efficient.

Star had to admit, there was plenty of fuel to be had
in the forest, compared to the buffalo chips and mea-
ger wood of the prairie. She carried armful after armful of dead branches and piled them near the campsite.

With each succeeding trip, she could see the struc-
ture taking shape. The others had lashed poles between stout saplings and were now beginning to apply
brush to the framework. It was not so unlike the
brush arbors of the People, after all, except for the
roof, which slanted sharply from the open south front
to the ground on the north side.

It was on her sixth or seventh foray into the woods
that she saw the deer. There were three of them,
standing in the shelter of a dense oak thicket. The big
buck stood motionless, large ears spread as he looked
straight at the intruder. Two does stood nearby.

Star was careful to continue her movements so as
not to disturb the animals. She gathered sticks, aware
of the animals' gaze, until she had moved out of their
sight. Then she hurried back to the camp.

"Come," she motioned to Traveler, "there are deer in the woods."

Quickly, he dropped the brush he was tying and picked up his bow.

"Where?"

"I will show you."

The two threaded their way through the trees, Star in the lead, careful not to alarm the animals. Finally they came to the clearing where she had seen them.

"Here," she signed. "In the oaks."

It took a moment to make out the outlines of the deer again, their color was so nearly that of the brown, dead leaves on the thicket behind them.

"There are three. One is lying down."

"I see."

Traveler drew his bow and the arrow twanged from the string. All three animals jumped and fled, crashing through the underbrush. Star turned to look at the bowman in disappointment, but there was a smile on his face.

"We have fresh meat tonight!" he signed.

He waited a few moments, then carefully led the way across the clearing. He scrutinized the ground, and finally pointed to a few drops of blood on a fallen oak leaf. He parted the foliage and led the way, occasionally pointing to more bloody smears as he passed.

They had gone less distance than a long bow shot when he pointed ahead. There lay a fat doe, the feathered end of Traveler's arrow protruding between the ribs.

He had fitted another arrow to the string and moved forward cautiously, but another shot was unnecessary. The animal was quite dead. The bow was laid aside, and he drew a short knife to begin butchering. Star wondered if he thought of the medicine knife. He would be using it now if he had not traded it for the girl. Of course, if he had not, she would not have found the deer, and he might not need the knife.

"Go and bring Plum Leaf," he motioned.

Star hurried back to camp and returned with the

other woman. Traveler had nearly removed the skin and now did so with the help of the others to roll the animal over. He spread the skin and they began to place choice cuts of meat on its flesh side.

The girl was a willing helper. Since early childhood she had assisted in the butchering of buffalo, and occasionally elk and deer. This was no different. Her assistance meant more and better food, so it was merely a matter of self-interest to do her part.

For the first time, Plum Leaf seemed to look at her with a quizzical half tolerance. Maybe, her expression said, maybe here is a useful helping hand. By the time they finished the major part of the drudgery, Plum Leaf was almost smiling.

The three moved back to the camp, each carrying a load of meat. Traveler carried the largest, wrapped in the skin of the animal.

Star was pleased that he had set the head up ceremoniously and addressed it in his own tongue. She did not understand the words, but was sure they resembled those of the medicine man's ceremony for the buffalo among the People.

My brother, we are sorry to kill you, but you are our life. As your flesh comes from the grass of the prairie, so our flesh comes from yours. We thank you for our lives.

This appeared to be a similar ceremony, and it gave her a warm feeling toward the couple who were now all she had.

They arrived at the camp, and Star resumed gathering wood while the others kindled a fire and finished the brush lodge. They were none too soon. By the time darkness fell, the first fluffy big flakes of snow were beginning to drift downward through the woods.

Star wondered if this couple knew what they were doing in building a brush lodge against the storm, with one side completely open. She hoped so, because this storm looked like Cold Maker's first big war party of the season.

The open-sided shelter proved adequate for its purpose. Star had to admit that the fire, close in front, warmed the little cavity quite well. It was like half of a skin-covered lodge, almost. The more snow that collected on the slanting brush shelter, the more windproof it became. Once Traveler rose to kick drifting snow against a drafty corner.

The three snuggled together in the shelter, sharing body warmth for comfort if not for survival. Star had only a slight reluctance to share the strangers' bed. The alternative was certainly to be avoided.

They had eaten well, which also helped provide warmth. Star decided, as she lay trying to sleep, that she had been more uncomfortable many times. Here she lay, listening to the snores of her captors, who were actually being relatively kind to her. Her belly was full, she was warm beneath the thick robe and between the warm bodies of the others. She would make the best of this captivity. She would learn all that she could, to better prepare her for the day she would escape.

She would start tomorrow, by beginning to learn the language of her captors. She drifted off to sleep, with the sound of falling snow hissing softly through the dry oak thicket.

11

» » »

Like most of Cold Maker's early probes into the warmer regions, this one was short-lived. It could be seen that Sun Boy was retaliating quickly and that in a day's time travel would again be practical.

"We stay today," Traveler announced in sign-talk. "Go tomorrow."

Plum Leaf began to work with part of the venison, slicing thin strips from the more tender cuts. These she placed on a rack contrived from green sticks and propped them near the fire. Star saw that this resembled the drying process used by the People. This method would produce partly cooked, partly dried, and partly smoked meat.

The girl began to assist in the preparation. She had not overlooked the tentative approval by Plum Leaf last evening. Now she would attempt to improve relations by being helpful.

Plum Leaf smiled and nodded, accepting Star's help.

"Mother, I would learn your tongue," Star signed after a while.

Plum Leaf appeared startled but pleased.

"Mine, or his?" she indicated her husband.

Star shrugged.

"Both, maybe. Which do you use together?"

"Both." The woman chuckled. "Mine, when we are with my people. His for his tribe. When we are alone, both, sometimes."

Aiee, thought Star, this would make it difficult. To learn one new tongue was bad enough.

She had quickly learned enough of the Head Splitters' language to converse with other children at the time of the annual Sun Dance. Looks Far had commented on her quickness. Of course, she now recalled, he and Blue Dawn had had different languages when they met. It seemed no problem to them.

Well, Star decided, she would attempt to learn enough of her captors' talk to be well-informed. That would make escape easier.

"We go now to your people?" the girl asked.

"Yes," Plum Leaf nodded. "They are three, maybe four sleeps south. We will winter there."

Star had been thinking about the winter since her discussion with Traveler. It was the major reason for her pledge not to escape. There was no use to flee into the uncertainty of a winter in a strange country. She would bide her time and choose the proper moment to escape in favorable weather next spring.

"Then what, after the winter?"

Plum Leaf shrugged.

"Back north, to his people."

Star nodded. It was enough for now. At some point in the journey back north, she would escape and make her way west into the plains. There she would have no trouble. Any village of Growers would have news of the People. They would know all the gossip of the area, including where the bands were camped. She might even encounter the Eastern band of the People. They often camped near the River of Swans, she knew, and she could request help from them until she could reach her own band.

But that was in the future. For now, she would learn

what she could from her captors. She studied the couple through that day as they moved in a leisurely fashion around the camp.

They were about the same age as her own parents, a few summers older, perhaps. Plum Leaf was an attractive woman, graying a little at the temples, with a hint of sadness around her eyes. The set of her lips, which Star had originally thought unpleasant, now seemed more like a reflection of disappointment. The girl wondered if hers had been a sad life. Perhaps it had been difficult for her, to follow her roving husband across the land. Had they aways done so?

"Have you had children?" Star asked impulsively.

The sad look deepened, and Plum Leaf's dark eyes took on a faraway gaze.

"Only one. She is dead," the woman spoke briefly.

Star uncomfortably realized that she had touched a sensitive area. Her cheeks burned with embarrassment. She was glad when, at that moment, Sun Boy chose to come out into the open. Warm rays reached out to touch and brighten the day.

Snow melted and dripped from the trees or gathered in puddles in low spots in the forest floor. Sun Boy's torch never failed to lift the spirits, and Star's thoughts were strong and good.

She thought much that day of the child that these people had lost. How old had the girl been? Was this the reason for their wandering, or had it always been so? Someday she would ask more.

The thing that she really wished to ask, of course, she dared not mention. She wished to know of the medicine knife, the shiny instrument that had been the price paid for her. She felt that not only had Plum Leaf disapproved of the trade, even Traveler himself had been dissatisfied. She must do her best to convince them that the bargain was a good one. Thus she would receive better treatment.

But above all, she wanted to know more of the medicine knife itself. Where had it come from? How had Traveler acquired it? Were there others like it?

The strange attraction took her thoughts one step further. The Elk-dog Medicine of the People had been brought from a far country by her ancestor, Heads Off. He had been of another tribe, who had had fur upon their faces. Even now, some of the men in her mother's family showed a heavy fringe on the cheeks and upper lip. They found it difficult to pluck with the clam-shell tweezers, and some even wore it proudly, as a mark of their heritage.

The questions that had bothered Star since she first saw the medicine knife dealt with the same phenomenon. If, as she suspected, the knife was of the same substance as the medicine bit, did it come from the same source? Did the shiny material come from only one place, like the red stone of medicine pipes?

More specifically, had the medicine knife that so excited her curiosity come originally from the hair-faced tribe of Heads Off, in some mysterious far-off land?

12

》》》

Pale Star stood on a hilltop outside the village, letting the wind stir her hair. She took deep breaths of the air, scenting the damp, musty hint of moist earth and growing things. It was the Moon of Awakening. Green sprigs of grass peeked through the brown of the forest floor or in the open meadows. Buds swelled on the maples, and the willows shone yellow-green in the sun.

She watched a long line of geese honking their way northward. They are going home, she told herself. Home, to their faraway north country to build whatever lodges geese build and raise their families. There was a homesick ache in her heart, yet a mixed feeling also.

As long as she could remember, Star had watched the geese each spring, longing to follow their path to new sights, sounds, and smells. She was unsure this season whether the restlessness that she felt was to return home to her people or to see the strange northern region that Traveler spoke of as home.

She took another deep sigh, filling her lungs with

the breath of springtime. She could hardly believe all that had happened to her in the past few moons: her abduction and captivity, the trading session in which she became the property of Traveler.

She marveled at how rapidly her relationship to this man and his wife, Plum Leaf, had changed. At first she had hated and resented them. They had been strict, but very quickly Star had realized that if she behaved in a cooperative manner, they treated her well.

She had learned much of their language. Both their languages, actually, as both spoke their own tongues. Star understood conversation fairly well, though she had some difficulty in speaking. However, it seemed more important to listen than to talk. She learned more. She was cautious not to reveal all of her knowledge of their language. It would be more effective if they thought she did not understand. To further this, the girl always accompanied her halting speech with hand-sign talk.

She had an odd feeling about this deceit. She felt almost guilty at times, as if she were not completely honest with the couple who had become her family. It had been apparent very quickly that for Traveler, the girl somehow replaced the child they had lost. Plum Leaf, though slower to let down her reserve, seemed to feel much the same.

In a short while, both had stopped regarding Star as a captive and were treating her like an honored daughter.

This helped the girl adjust to a strange and repugnant way of life through the winter. They had reached the village of Plum Leaf's people, and Star found it as she had feared. They lived in permanent lodges with solid sides made of logs and mud. To her consternation, there was no way out except the door.

It was with a feeling that bordered on panic that she entered the lodge of Plum Leaf's relatives, where they would spend the winter. It was dark and smoky and smelled of body odors and sweat, a heavy animal smell

like that of a bear's den. Star could barely refrain from
rushing back outside in terror.

Cold Maker helped her adjust to this sort of living.
At least the lodge was warm. However, the girl for the
rest of her life would never completely overcome the
threat of confining walls and the absence of the fresh
prairie winds that purified the air of a skin-covered
lodge.

It was to escape this sense of confinement that she
would go to the hilltop when the weather permitted.
She had found the spot before the severe thrust of
winter descended. Here, at least, she could see a far
horizon, though not the grassy vistas of the prairie.
Here she would think, dream, and plan.

A part of the plan was always her escape and return
to the People. Many times she lived the event in her
imagination. She would inform Traveler that their
agreement was at an end. He would, possibly, try to
talk her out of an attempted escape. He might even tie
her at night, as he had done at first.

But she would escape. There was no doubt whatever
in her mind on that point. At some time in their
travels, when the situation was right, she would strike
out to the west and home.

Sometimes she imagined instead that she would
explain her need to Traveler and Plum Leaf. She would
convince them to return with her. They would meet
her parents, who would give them gifts in the happiness of their daughter's safe return. It was not a dream
that was entirely out of the question. After all, Traveler's obvious preoccupation as a wanderer and trader
might make such a scheme interesting to him.

By far her most prominent fantasy, however, continued to be escape. When the time was right, she
would know.

The major event of the winter, aside from her adjust-
ment to her new surroundings, was her coming of age.
She had seen and felt the changes in her body. Her
budding breasts became larger and fuller, assuming a
womanly size and conformation. Slim hips became

more rounded, accenting her slender waist. Her long, muscular legs began to assume softer lines. The calves swelled slightly, contrasting with slim ankles and smoothly rounded thighs.

Star was pleased with her appearance, realizing her attractiveness. She welcomed admiring glances from some of the young men, though she saw none who really interested her.

She was amused when one elderly man approached Traveler in an attempt to buy her. The anger in the face of the man who now considered her a foster daughter was so intense that the prospective buyer had departed quickly. It was apparent in his look of indignation as he drew his robe around him that he did not understand at all. He had offered the trader a fair price and had been rebuffed. The two men parted in mutual anger and dislike.

Star was not surprised when her arrival at womanhood was heralded by her first menstruation. Plum Leaf accompanied her to the menstrual lodge and explained the customs of the tribe.

"You will stay here until you are no longer unclean. Is it not so among your own people, child?"

"Yes, of course. But there is no special lodge. A woman stays in her own lodge."

"But what of the risk to others?"

Pale Star shrugged.

"Of course, she must take care not to touch certain things," she explained. "Her husband's weapons, his food."

"Yes, that would be a risk," agreed Plum Leaf. "Sometimes a bow never shoots straight again. But you have no menstrual lodge at all?"

"None. Some tribes do this, but not ours. Our women are careful not to threaten others."

It was with a degree of pride that Star stated the position of women among her people. The slightly critical interpretation was not lost on Plum Leaf, but she chose not to pursue it. She only clucked her tongue disapprovingly and walked on.

It was only after a few days in the menstrual lodge that Star began to see the custom in proper perspective. There were, after all, some advantages.

She knew that menstrual taboos varied from one tribe to another. The principle was always the same. If a bow or other weapon was touched by an unclean woman, its effectiveness was impaired. There were stories of calamities resulting from accidental contacts of this sort.

She had always viewed with disapproval the menstrual-lodge custom of the People's allies, the Head Splitters. Women in her own tribe held high status, and it seemed barbaric to banish a woman from normal society for the reason of her menses.

Now, in the relaxed surroundings of the special lodge, she began to feel a sisterhood with the other women there. They visited, laughed, made jokes about their husbands, and had a generally good time during their stay away from responsibility. Star did not understand all the innuendos of the talk in a tongue she was only learning, but she enjoyed being part of it.

Even more, she began to see great advantages in the custom. There was a young woman in the lodge when Star came there who apparently had a poor marriage. She talked about her husband's shortcomings, his family, and his disposition. Several days later, when some of the earlier inhabitants had already left the lodge, Star realized that White Fawn was still there.

It was not until someone made a comment that Star realized what was happening.

"Fawn, how long will your husband believe your time is still here?"

Everyone laughed, and the young woman tossed her head insolently.

"As long as I tell him."

The other women laughed again. Even so, White Fawn gathered her belongings and moved out the following day.

Still, there had been planted the seed of an idea in the mind of Pale Star. A woman could, within reasonable limits, declare when she chose to stay in the menstrual lodge. If she did not blatantly abuse the custom, she could retain complete control of her body and her sexuality. This would be good to remember.

Another flock of geese winged their way north overhead, their noisy clatter bringing her back to the present. Traveler was climbing the hill to stand beside her.

Together they watched the long lines of graceful birds disappear into the blue of distance. It was only then that he spoke.

"It is time to go home, little one."

"Yes," she answered softly.

She did not voice the rest of her thought. They might agree on the time to move, but their distant goals might be quite different.

"Yes," Star whispered to herself. "It is time to go home."

13

>> >> >>

Star tried to think the situation through as they traveled. It would soon be time to make her move, if she could assure herself of the right moment.

Once more, she returned in her thinking to the time of her abduction. From that point they had traveled, as nearly as she could remember, seven or eight sleeps. Then had been the trade, when she became the property of Traveler. One more day to the east, then four sleeps south to the village of Plum Leaf's people.

Or had that been more of a southeasterly direction? It was extremely frustrating not to see Sun Boy until he was well in his day's run. She still had the occasional feeling that the forest was closing in. Who would choose to live in such a country, she asked herself irritably, where one cannot even see earth's rim?

She had decided that her best method to observe direction was to observe the stars at night. The circling Seven Hunters could usually be found, wheeling on their nightly journey around their lodge at the Real-star. That, at least, was constant. Sometimes as darkness fell, she would be surprised at the Real-star's position. Then she would mentally curse the wandering trails that meandered through the woods around hills, destroying her sense of direction. She would spend a time reorienting herself and estimating her position in reference to the Sacred Hills of home, far to the west.

In this way, Pale Star kept count of their progress. At the beginning of the journey north, she had decided that twenty sleeps, perhaps, would take them as far as she should go before her move to the west. Allowing for days when their progress was slow, and those when they did not move at all, she felt that she should escape before the next moon.

Now, that time was at hand. The Moon of Awakening had given way to the Moon of Greening, and the trees were in full leaf. That, Star decided, was a mixed advantage. It would be easier to hide from pursuit when she made her break. It also made it more difficult, however, for her to establish direction. There were entire days when she did not see the sky. Sometimes it seemed to her that the heavy, damp air of the deep woodlands would choke her. Almost in tears, she would long for the open sweep of clean prairie breezes.

Just now, she followed along the trail, seeing the back of Traveler's pack ahead of her. Behind her, she was aware of the footsteps of Plum Leaf. It would be a good day's travel, Star knew. Good, that is, from the standpoint of Traveler. He would be pleased that they had come so far.

It was, perhaps, not so good for Pale Star. They were coming close to the point where she must turn westward or retrace much distance when she did make her move.

Yes, it was time. Tonight, while Traveler was in good humor from a successful day, she would inform him that their bargain was at an end. Even so, it was none too soon. He might watch her very closely for a time, preventing her escape. And, of course, each day's travel took them farther from the People. She must tell him immediately.

Strange, she thought. Why do I dread this? She had postponed the confrontation, at first for good and logical reasons. Then there seemed to be things that prevented such a move. They were camped in an uncomfortable shelter against the rain, and it did not seem right. Again, they stopped for a day with a village of Growers, and the entire time was spent in smoking, trading, and storytelling. There was no opportunity to approach Traveler.

Now, she had finally admitted that she was avoiding the time when she must tell him. It would hurt him and hurt Plum Leaf also.

Star realized that these kind people must dread the moment when she rejected her pledge not to escape. They had settled into a routine that seemed to deny any friction at all. They seemed intent on believing that Star had always been a part of them, the daughter they had lost.

This situation bothered the girl even more because she, too, felt it. She found herself feeling disloyal as she plotted escape. Disloyal, like an errant daughter who lacked respect for her elders.

She shook her head angrily. Why should she have such feelings? It was ridiculous. She was a captive, and must escape to return to her people.

She panted a little as she shifted her pack and set her foot firmly to climb an irregular portion of the trail. Ahead of her on the hillside, Traveler glanced back to see the progress of the women.

"We will stop soon," he called.

Rivulets of sweat ran down her face, stinging her eyes and tasting of salt in her mouth. She struggled up the broken hillside, irritated with herself. If she worked this hard at anything, it should be for a good reason. This effort should be used for escape.

Yes, it was definitely time to recant her promise and escape as soon as possible. She glanced at the sky and saw that it would soon be time to stop for the night. The halt mentioned by Traveler as he called down the hill would be to camp, not just for a rest stop.

That would be the place, she promised herself. Tonight the night. She would talk to Traveler and let him know. He could expect her attempted escape at any time after that.

Behind her, Star could hear the heavy breathing of Plum Leaf as the older woman struggled up the hill. This decision would be very hard for her.

Once more, the girl thought of the possibility of asking them to visit her people. Yes, that would be it! She could tell them that the agreement was at an end and at the same time invite them to accompany her, rather than just announce her intent to escape.

Pleased, Star renewed her efforts and gained some distance on Traveler as she climbed. They topped the ridge, and the trail dropped away before them, still winding among the trees.

Traveler pointed ahead. A clear spring bubbled out of the rock, and a pleasant clearing offered a good camping place for the night.

"Here!" Traveler called, shrugging his pack from his shoulder.

He dropped the load to the ground in a clump of fragrant ferns that surrounded the base of a massive sycamore. Panting heavily, Star tossed her pack also and stepped to the spring to drink.

The water was clear and icy cold, and they drank deeply. Star looked around and started to speak to the other woman, but she had not yet arrived.

"Where is Plum Leaf?" her husband asked.

Star shrugged.

"She was right behind me when we crossed the ridge."

The two sprang back up the trail together, Traveler in the lead, calling his wife's name in alarm.

Near the top of the ridge sat Plum Leaf, breathing heavily. Her pack had fallen to the ground.

"I am all right," she protested. "I just stopped to rest."

It was obviously more. Her face was ashen, her breath was coming in ragged gasps. Occasionally there was a catch in her breathing, followed by a paroxysm of dry coughing. Traveler stooped to lift her, and Star picked up the pack.

They moved slowly down the trail, Traveler in the lead, half-carrying the sick woman.

"Why did you say nothing?" he scolded.

"I am all right," Plum Leaf repeated weakly. "I will be strong when I have rested a little."

Star knew better. The woman appeared quite ill. How could they have overlooked the labored breath, the dry cough? The girl now realized that for the past day or two Plum Leaf had not been at her best. She had lagged behind, catching up at the rest stops. Star felt guilty that she had not noticed.

Another thought came to her. It would be impossible now to speak to Traveler about her pledge. She could not do so under these circumstances. Plum Leaf would need her help to recover.

14

» » »

The next day was gray and dreary, like the spirits of the travelers who camped at the spring.

Plum Leaf insisted that she was all right, but the cough and shortness of breath worsened. Once in the night, Star had awakened to find the other woman shaking with a chill. Her teeth chattered uncontrollably, though the night was actually quite warm.

Star longed for the advice of her uncle Looks Far. He would know of treatment for this strange malady. There would be something, some plant to use, some song or incantation, that would make her well.

Even as she thought this, the girl wondered if Looks Far could help, if he were here. His medicine was of the prairie, with different plants and herbs. Each area must have its own medicine, she reflected. Strange, she had never thought of that.

If, then, they could only transport the sick woman to the Sacred Hills, where Looks Far would heal her. Star gazed into the fire, lost in thought.

"What are you thinking, little one?" Traveler interrupted.

"It is nothing, Uncle," answered the girl, using the People's term of respect. "I only wished that we could take Plum Leaf to my kinsman, Looks Far. He is a skilled medicine man."

Interest lighted the sad, tired face of Traveler.

"Where are your people?"

"I do not know. They move around the prairie, you know."

"Yes. How far to your country?"

The girl shrugged.

"Maybe twenty sleeps. But, then, we would still have to find them."

"Too far," nodded Traveler. "It would be no closer than her own people. I thought of turning back. But it is too far. We cannot carry her."

"Are there other tribes near here?"

"Yes, but I do not know where."

"Uncle, do you know of the plants in this forest? What would they use?"

Traveler shrugged helplessly.

"This place is not my home, the plants and trees are different. And I know little of such things, anyway."

Pale Star had never seen him so depressed. His whole attitude seemed hopeless. Surely something could be done.

"Do you recognize any plants at all?"

Traveler shook his head sadly.

"None for this."

Star was desperate. She tried to think of a similar situation among the People. What had been done?

Dimly, she remembered a time when she herself had been very ill. She remembered her mother cradling her in strong arms and feeding her broth with a horn spoon. Then, later, the rolled bites of pounded hackberries mixed with buffalo fat.

She had seen hackberry trees on the trail. Could any still hold a few dried fruits from last season? Or would another berry of some sort suffice?

"Uncle," she said, "I have a thought. Something used among my people. I will make soup, and then we must find some hackberries, or something like that. Are there others here? I want to pound them with fat."

She did not specify buffalo fat. She knew that would be better, but there would be none. Maybe the fat of a deer would work.

Traveler brightened.

"Yes," he said, "I had forgotten. My people use the fruit of the rose for this."

As soon as it was light, Traveler went to search for useful ingredients. The season was wrong, but something might be found. Fresh meat, too, would be valuable.

Star was glad to see him show some interest. She had become quite concerned about his loss of spirit.

She dug a small pit near the fire, to use in cooking, and then rose.

"I am going to find cooking stones," she told Plum Leaf.

"From the hillside," warned Plum Leaf, panting from the exertion of speaking. "Those from near a stream have water spirits."

"Of course, Mother," Star smiled and stroked the hot forehead. "It is the same in my country."

Plum Leaf drifted to sleep as the girl went to look for stones. It was true about the water spirits. A tortured spirit, placed in the fire, would break free of its stone with a loud explosion. It could be quite dangerous.

She hoped that Traveler could find a deer. It was possible to use a dried skin from one of the packs to line her cooking pit, but it was a nuisance. Besides, the soup made in a freshly killed skin was more nourishing.

It was nearly midday before they had assembled the necessary ingredients. Traveler had managed to kill a deer.

"There is little fat," he apologized. "The season is wrong."

Star nodded and took the skin to line her cooking pit. The meat was laid aside for the moment. She partially filled the pit with water, added meat and some onions she had found near the spring, and placed her cooking stones in the fire.

As a stone became hot enough to hiss when a drop of water was splashed on it, she would pick it up with willow tongs and drop it into the water. Cool stones were removed and placed back in the fire.

The stew began to simmer as hot stones were added. Fragrant steam rose in a puff with each added stone. Plum Leaf awoke and showed a little interest.

Traveler handed a wooden cup to Star, who dipped broth from the simmering pit to allow it to cool. Very gently and carefully, she began to feed sips to the sick woman.

"It is good, Star."

The girl nodded.

"It will make you strong."

Traveler had also brought part of the liver of the deer. Through the next day, they cooked this nourishing flesh and crumbled it with melted fat and a few rose berries.

"It will help her strength," Star said confidently.

Traveler nodded. The restorative properties of fresh liver were well known.

Star remembered the excitement of the first buffalo kills of springtime, at home on the prairie. Everyone would have become tired of the sameness of dried and stored supplies, and a real hunger for fresh meat developed.

The Moon of Hunger, it was called, just before Awakening. Originally, an alternate name had been the Moon of Starvation, as food ran short. With the coming of the horse, it was said, there was enough food for all. There were jokes about finding a new name for the Moon of Hunger.

Gradually, the understanding changed. The hunger was not simply from lack of food. It was a deeper hunger, a craving for freshness, for the strong medicine of the buffalo. The animals carried in their bodies the massive strength, the life-spirit, stored from the richness of the grass they consumed.

"They bring the grass and the sun north when they come," Looks Far had told her. "They have eaten well through the winter, far to the south. Now, they bring the medicine to us."

She remembered the custom of her people, to eat fresh warm bites of the liver as they butchered. She had done it herself and rejoiced in the smell and taste of medicine that had been missing through the long months of the winter.

Now, Star applied these memories to the present situation. It could do no harm to feed the strength-giving medicine to the ailing woman. She tried it herself first, a small strip of raw liver. It was not as good as fresh buffalo liver, still warm from the kill, but perhaps it would help. She cut a small bite and fed it to Plum Leaf.

The older woman took it with surprise and chewed almost eagerly. She looked for another bite.

For three days they stayed at the spring, with Plum Leaf hovering between better and worse. They spent most of their waking hours either hunting food, preparing it, or feeding the sick woman. There were times when Star was ready to give up in despair, but she kept on, trying different combinations. She wished that she knew more of the incantations used by her uncle in such cases.

The sun rose on the fourth day and found Pale Star still sleeping from exhaustion. She had been up during the night, ministering to Plum Leaf.

Traveler shook her gently to waken her. There was a broad smile on his face as she opened her eyes to look at him.

"Wake up, little one," he spoke softly. "Your medicine has worked. She is better."

15

>> >> >>

It was true. There was a light in the eye of Plum Leaf that had not been there before, a color in her cheeks.

She still coughed, but now the cough was for a purpose, clearing the evil from her lungs and opening the passageways to fresh, life-giving air. It seemed that they could watch her grow stronger.

Of course, it was another three days before she became strong enough to travel. Even then, progress was slow. Star now brought up the rear, carefully watching the condition of the woman ahead. Sometimes she called ahead to Traveler and they paused for a rest.

Star had all but forgotten her determination to escape as soon as possible. Occasionally she thought of it but quickly assured herself that it was out of the question at this time. Plum Leaf needed her.

Their roles seemed reversed, almost. It was the younger woman who was now making decisions about their campsite for the night, about when to call for a needed rest stop. If, at the end of a tiring day, Plum

Leaf appeared more exhausted than usual, it was Star who hovered over her, to comfort her, feed her, and bring her water.

Traveler allowed this to happen without comment. It was as if, after the time of his wife's acute illness, he refused to look at the situation objectively. He was cheerful and optimistic, but it seemed sometimes that he was unwilling to see anything but what he wished to be.

He was cooperative. When Star felt that they should halt because Plum Leaf needed the rest, he willingly did so. He continued, however, to ignore the fact that his wife was not really gaining much strength. Their best days of travel were none too good, and each told heavily on Plum Leaf. At the end of a hard day, Star could see a hint of the ashen color, the heavy breathing, and the dilated nostrils as the lungs labored for breath.

Once she tried to talk to Traveler about it, but he brushed such talk aside.

"She is strong," he insisted. "She will do better in the north country."

Traveler seemed to think of the couple in terms of their younger years, in their beginnings together. It was part of his denial of reality, somehow, a denial that anything at all was wrong. A denial, actually, that they were no longer young, with the world before them.

"Besides," Traveler tossed out as an afterthought, "soon we will travel by water, and that will be easier."

For a moment, Star wondered if the man had lost his mind completely.

"*By water*? How can this be, Uncle?"

"We will get a canoe."

The word was unfamiliar to Star, and she requested more information. Resorting to hand-sign talk, she asked again.

"How is this called?"

Traveler responded with a hand-sign, a symbol for "boat." This became even more confusing. Boats, though rare, were not unknown to the People. Some tribes they knew occasionally used a skin boat to cross a river.

But she did not see how people could travel in such a thing. They were usually made of the skin of a large bull, turned up at the edges and laced to a hoop of willow. One or possibly two people could sit in such a thing, pushing it along with poles. She could see no way in which it could actually be used to travel. She sought out Plum Leaf.

"Mother, Traveler says we will travel by water. Can this be?"

"Of course, child. His people do so almost entirely."

"Aiee! They have no elk-dogs?"

"Yes, but by water is easier."

Star had wondered about this, why the Forest People seemed to have no concern for horses. She had finally realized that it would be difficult to ride through the woods on horseback. A rider would constantly be in danger from overhanging limbs and the close quarters of the thick woods. But she had never heard of travel by water. It sounded slow and cumbersome. Well, if both her companions said so, it must be the custom, though she still had doubts. She would wait and see.

The country was changing as they traveled. The densely wooded hills were behind them, and now large areas of forest were interspersed with expanses of prairie. It made Star pleased and at the same time homesick to identify prairie plants familiar to her. She could see the dried seed heads of last year's grass and recognize real-grass, plume-grass, and several of the smaller types. She wondered if the country of Traveler's people was mostly woods or mostly prairie. Finally she asked as they stopped to rest.

"Both," was the terse reply, "and water, too."

"Water, Uncle? I do not understand."

"Big rivers," Traveler grunted in explanation. "Lakes. Big water."

Once more there was a problem of language. Star's

experience did not include the memory of a really large body of water. There were few lakes in the territory of the People. The Big River, in the northern portion of the area, was still no more than a long bow shot in width. The term "big water" that Traveler used was almost meaningless to her. Well, she would wait and see.

It was not until they came to the river that she began to realize a hint of what Traveler meant. Immediately, she saw that this river was far wider than any she had seen.

Like others of the People, Star was a good swimmer, but she would have hesitated to attempt to swim across this stream. Only a distant line of willows and the occasional taller cottonwoods marked the far shore.

"*Aiee!*" she half whispered to herself.

She turned to Traveler.

"How do we cross?"

Traveler laughed.

"We do not. This is the trail!"

Slowly, Star realized that he was serious. He meant to take them on the surface of this river in a boat of some sort. A knot tightened in the pit of her stomach. The current was swift and muddy, brownish gray with the silt of flooded streams far upriver. Melting snows many sleeps away must be the cause.

Large logs, trees, and assorted driftwood swirled past. Star watched a large rounded object float toward them, finally identifying it as a bloated buffalo carcass.

Traveler wished to take them on this hideous expanse of foul water? She could hardly believe it. She almost recoiled in terror at the thought of murky depths and the evil spirits that might lurk there to clutch at unwary swimmers.

She glanced at Traveler again, who was still smiling broadly. He indicated the river with a sweep of his hand.

"Is this not beautiful?"

The girl stood in shocked silence. It is good, she reflected, that everyone's medicine is not the same.

16

>> >> >>

They traveled along the river for two more days before they reached the village that Traveler sought. Plum Leaf was tiring very easily, making frequent rest stops necessary.

Star dreaded their arrival at the village. She knew that there would be rest for the ailing Plum Leaf, but Traveler had also promised that here they would find a boat in which to travel. She was increasingly apprehensive about that.

There was also the doubt about what sort of people these might be, what their lodges were like, their customs. Her companions seemed to think nothing of it, but of course they traveled and were in contact with other tribes frequently.

"We have friends here," Traveler had said.

Their first glimpse of any of the natives proved a surprise to Star. Traveler, walking in the lead, said nothing but merely pointed to the river. There, halfway across, were two people, apparently sitting in the water. Quickly the girl realized that they must be in a boat of some sort, perhaps the type mentioned by Traveler.

The two in the boat apparently saw the travelers at about the same time. Star could not see their craft very well, but could tell that it rode very low in the water. The men each picked up a short stick from the bottom of the boat and began to thrust them into the water.

Star was amazed. The light craft seemed to leap forward like a fish, skimming across the surface with remarkable speed. Even more amazing, their progress was upstream, directly into the current. Now she realized that their sticks were not used for poling the boat along but for stroking against the pressure of the water. She could see that the sticks were flattened, like a larger version of a noisemaking toy used by children of the People. The toy, swung rapidly by a thong, produced its sound by fluttering against the wind.

This was much the same, Star thought, except that the wing-shaped sticks were used to push against the water. Yes, her first thought that this boat resembled a fish was a good one. The motion of the men's sticks as they stroked the water was much like swimming.

Traveler interrupted her thoughts.

"They are from the village. They go to tell the others."

There was a moment of anxiety until Star remembered that this was a village where Traveler was known and had friends. They moved on along the trail, as the canoe slid out of sight around the river's next bend.

The first people they encountered merely stared curiously. They were accompanied by an assortment of barking dogs. Some things never change, Star reflected.

A young man stepped forward with a smile and a greeting. The language was strange, but it was apparent that Traveler understood.

"This is the chief's son," he explained to Star. "He comes to bring welcome."

As they encountered more people, a number called to Traveler in greeting. He was apparently well known and respected here. Some accompanied their greeting with hand-signs, so Star was able to follow the general idea. They were asking if Traveler had come to trade, what he had brought, what he was seeking.

Star glanced at him. Traveler seemed a different person, glowing with excitement and challenge. He was no longer the depressed, anxious man he had been at times on the trail. This was his world, the excitement of new places, new people, new things to trade.

"We will stay here a few days," Traveler observed. "It will be good."

Yes, thought Star, it will be good, but not for reasons Traveler might think. She was increasingly concerned for Plum Leaf, and it would be good for her to rest. The girl had the uncomfortable feeling that Traveler was still denying the seriousness of his wife's condition. At any rate, it would be good to rest.

The path widened as they came to a cluster of lodges. The structures were rectangular, built of poles and logs and thatched with grass. They were, as Star had feared, permanently situated, and once more she wondered how people could live this way. There was the heavy animal smell of people everywhere, mixed this time with a new and different odor, that of fish. There were racks of drying or smoke-curing fish along the path between the lodges.

Star wondered for a moment if each tribe could be identified by its own smell. She would have to speak to Looks Far about that when she returned home. He would be interested in her observations.

Another odd thing caught her attention. At intervals, hanging from poles and trees, were clusters of large gourds, each with a round hole in one side. Glossy black-purple birds wheeled and fluttered around these areas, sometimes entering the gourds, apparently to feed young.

"These gourds are the lodges of birds?" Star asked in wonder.

Traveler nodded.

"Yes, the people make lodges so the birds will stay here."

"But, why?"

"They eat flies and—."

Star did not understand his last words. It was the language problem again. She resorted to sign-talk and determined that he referred to the flying insects that breed in stagnant puddles and emerge to bite at dusk. She could see the usefulness of the bird lodges. Anything that would reduce the hordes of tiny biting creatures in the damp of the river's course would be welcome.

"Ho!" someone called.

They turned to see a sign-talk question from the crowd.

"Will there be stories tonight?"

"Of course," Traveler signed in answer. "Bring your friends!"

Star began to see Traveler's method. He would attract a crowd with his stories and use the resulting interest to carry on his bartering.

The young man who had first greeted them pointed ahead and ushered them into a somewhat larger lodge. It appeared to be a meeting place.

"We will stay here," Traveler told the girl.

He shrugged his pack aside and set it against the wall. He turned to Plum Leaf.

"Are you all right?"

His wife nodded weakly and sat down. Star spread a robe for her to be on and arranged their belongings nearby.

"You two stay here," Traveler was saying. "I must go and give our respects to the chief."

He rummaged in a pack for a small gift to offer.

"You will be safe," he added for the benefit of the anxious girl. "We are guests here."

17

» » »

The story fire burned bright, driving shadows back into the darkness at the edge of the trees. The river murmured a soft whisper, unseen beyond the village.

A crowd had gathered to hear the stories of the visitor. Traveler told his tales skillfully, with suspense and emotion. Star had watched him do this before but had not been so impressed. Of course, at that time she had been a prisoner, hating and resenting everything that happened.

With shocked surprise, she reminded herself that she was *still* a prisoner. Somehow, it did not seem so now. She was interested, eager to hear Traveler's stories, and to see how they would be received. She found herself wishing him well.

He must be a very good storyteller. He had captivated the interest of the Forest people. Star had understood little of his talk and cared less at the time.

Now she watched closely while the crowd settled into silence and Traveler rose to begin. Star wondered what language he would use. She would not be able to follow the story in the tongue of their hosts.

To her relief, the storyteller used hand-sign talk in addition. This helped immensely. He was really a skillful speaker, as she had remembered. She was reminded of the storytellers among her own people, and the tales they could tell around the fires. Some were scary, some happy, others funny or serious.

One of the greatest storytellers of the People, it was said, had been her ancestor, Eagle, son of Heads Off. Eagle had been able to tell the stories of long-ago times as if he had actually been there. Star had sometimes regretted that she had never known him. Still, the storytelling tradition ran strong in her family, and she listened with interest.

Traveler was telling of why the bobcat's tail is short, to the delight of his audience. The spotted cat's tail was once long, he explained. It had frozen tightly to the ice when a sudden change in weather occurred while Cat was drinking. Many solutions were tried before he finally elected to sacrifice the tail to free himself.

The listeners rocked with laughter. Then their chief rose.

"It is good, Traveler," chuckled Hunts-In-The-Rain. "Here is our story."

He then told how Spotted Cat was instructed at the time of creation to be a night hunter and never to show himself in daylight. One night he stayed out too long, and was just hurrying into his den as the sun rose. An eagle, mistaking the dragging tail for a small furry creature, swooped down and snatched it off. Cat is still a night hunter, almost, and still has a short tail.

The audience chuckled appreciatively at the familiar tale. Star enthusiastically nodded. This would be an amusing evening.

Hunts-In-The-Rain was speaking to Traveler as the crowd began to quiet again. Then both turned to Star.

"The chief wishes to know," Traveler asked, "if your people's story is the same as mine."

Star shook her head.

"No. Tell him it is different."

The two men conversed further, and Traveler turned back again.

"He wishes to hear your story."

"But I do not speak his tongue!"

"Use sign-talk."

The listeners were becoming restless. Star rose, embarrassed, and faced their host.

"My chief," she began in hand-signals, "I speak none of your tongue, but I will try."

Hunts-In-The-Rain nodded and relaxed for the story.

"In long-ago times," Star began, "Spotted Cat had a long tail, as you know."

Everyone smiled seriously.

"In my country, among my people, there is a legend of the Old Man of the Shadows. He is a trickster, who can help or hurt. You have such a trickster?" she asked the chief.

"Not quite, but we know of him."

"Yes. Well, the Old Man had changed himself to a hollow tree, and Spotted Cat hid inside. But Old Man played a trick. He made a knothole behind, and Cat's tail hung out."

With her hands she made the shape of the knothole, with a finger waggling through to represent the tail. The crowd was chuckling already.

"A hunter passed by and saw the fine fur of the tail. He chopped it off to decorate his bow case. There has been fur on bow cases ever since."

The listeners rocked with laughter over the double twist at the story's end. Star sat down.

"Stand up," motioned Traveler, seeing a good thing in this new interest.

Hunts-In-The-Rain smiled and nodded.

"Where are your people?" he questioned.

"Far to the west, my chief, in the Sacred Hills."

"How are they called?"

"We call ourselves 'the People.' Some call us Elk-dog people."

The old chief nodded.

Now a new idea struck Traveler.

"Star," he asked, "would you tell us of your people's beginnings?"

He had no idea of the story she might tell, but he recognized a natural storyteller. Even in sign-talk, the girl captivated her audience.

Star shrugged, still embarrassed by the attention.

"This, too, tells of the Old Man," she began.

The audience smiled and nodded.

"He brought my people into the world, from inside the earth. It was soon after Creation, and they were inside. Old Man sat on a hollow cottonwood log and tapped it with a stick. First Man and First Woman crawled through to the outside."

A murmur of approval went around the circle. It was a good Creation story. Star waited. Someone should now ask the obvious question. Would they overlook it because of the language difference? No, a young man was rising.

"Tell us," he signed, "are they still coming through?"

The crowd chuckled. This was part of the game, to attempt to catch the storyteller in a contradiction.

But Star was ready. An uninitiated listener would usually ask this question, and it was a trap.

"Of course not," she signed with an indignant frown. "The third person was a fat woman. She got stuck in the log, and no one has been through since!"

The listeners were delighted, not only at the story but that the joke was on one of their number. They howled with laughter, and hooted derisively at the young man who had asked the question.

The stories went on until far into the night. Traveler was delighted to have the village in such a good mood. It would help him to do well with the trading tomorrow.

He also was looking at Pale Star in a new light. She was already like a daughter to him, but he had overlooked how useful the girl might be. In one evening she had become very popular with these people. A

bright, attractive, and intelligent young woman could
be of great help in the bartering.

He would teach her. This girl could very quickly
learn when to introduce a sympathetic smile, a friendly
glance, perhaps a suggestion of a more lenient trade
into the barter. He felt that she would enjoy it, even.

Star's excited thoughts were much the same. She
had enjoyed the attention, the laughter at her jokes. It
was apparent that she had been helpful to Traveler
this evening. But now she wished to return to where
Plum Leaf rested, to see how she felt.

Traveler was calling to the crowd.

"Now we must rest, my friends. We have traveled
far. Tomorrow we will trade. I have many fine things.
Knives, arrow points, tobacco. And we will need a
canoe!"

The crowd began to break up. Many people smiled
and nodded to Pale Star. She felt good.

Then a strange thing happened. With dozens of eyes
upon her as she smiled and waved, she suddenly felt a
stare from behind. The feeling was so powerful that
she turned quickly to see who was near. There was a
very real threat in the air, a warning of danger.

There was a cluster of young men, lounging against
the side of a nearby lodge. All were idly looking her
way, but the gaze of one in particular caught her
glance. It was a predatory look that made her skin
crawl and the hairs prickle on the back of her neck.

She had seen that look before, and for a moment
could not remember where. Then it came to her with
a chill. She had once chanced to see a large blue-black
snake as it crawled slowly into a nest of baby birds.
The cold glitter of the expressionless eyes and unsmil-
ing lips had been shocking.

Yet that was the expression on the face of this
young man. Star shuddered and turned away.

18

» » »

Star slept little that night. Plum Leaf was resting well, and Traveler was snoring. The girl lay on her robe, staring into the blackness of the lodge's thatch overhead, listening to the night sounds.

She could not rid herself of the feeling of dread that the insolent stare of the young warrior had evoked. She did not object to admiring glances. She had received many of them in this village. That was actually rather pleasing to a young woman, to be noticed.

But that was different somehow. Those had been smiling, friendly looks of admiration. Of desire, even. None had had the cold, scheming, covetous stare of this one. She shuddered and drew her robe around her against a chill that was not entirely that of the night air.

Destructive. That was it. Sheer, wanton destruction, without care for persons or things. She dreaded even seeing the man again.

Finally she slept, only to dream of the thin cruel lips and dark stare again. She awoke in a cold sweat, frightened yet angry at herself for the fright. She had

been through much in the past year. Why should this
incident have upset her so?

She was to find out next day. The village was awake
at daylight, stirring night fires into life and beginning
to cook. Star and Plum Leaf prepared food in a brush
arbor outside the lodge. People waved and nodded,
making the visitors welcome.

By the time they had eaten and were ready to trade,
the village teemed with life. People began to gather, to
trade or just to watch.

There was a brisk interest in arrow points, discussion of relative merits of blue-gray, red, or white stone,
from different areas. The shiny black stone was highly
prized, and Traveler had some good examples. Most of
the early trading, however, involved offering small
items for some of the trader's tobacco.

Star and Plum Leaf helped him spread out his wares
for display and answered questions. It was almost
midday when Star looked up and unexpectedly encountered the cruel eyes and snakelike lips of the
previous evening. She was too startled to react.

The man stared at her a moment, then stepped over
to confront Traveler.

"I am called 'Three Owls,' " he began in sign-talk,
by way of introduction.

"What is your tribe?" Traveler signed back. "You
are not of these people."

"No," the other replied. "I am a visitor here."

Star and Plum Leaf stared in fascination. There was
complete quiet. The onlookers somehow felt the ten-
sion in the air, though no one seemed to understand
it. Even Hunts-In-The-Rain, who sat nearby, seemed
at a loss.

"I would trade," continued the newcomer, ignoring
the question about his tribe. "You want a canoe. I
have one."

Traveler was still suspicious. He glanced from Three
Owls to another man who seemed to be his companion.

"What is your tribe?" he signed again.

"It does not matter. Do you wish to trade?"

Traveler spread his hands to indicate his trade goods displayed on robes in front of him.

"What do you want for your canoe?"

Three Owls smiled an oily smile in which there was no humor at all.

"A small thing only. The girl."

He pointed at Star.

Traveler's face darkened, but he maintained his composure. With great effort, he managed a smile.

"No," he signed, "she is not for sale."

"Everything has a price," purred Three Owls. "She is not your wife?"

"She is my daughter."

"No, she is of another tribe. I know that. You bought her, so there is no reason you could not sell her."

"But I will not."

Traveler was becoming furious.

"I only want to help you," Three Owls signed. "We have a canoe and offer a good trade to a fellow northerner. The girl can tell us stories and warm our beds."

Traveler sprang to his feet, reaching for his knife. The other man dropped to a fighting crouch, and people scattered.

"Stop!"

The ringing voice of Hunts-In-The-Rain spoke in his own tongue as he stepped between the combatants. There was no mistaking his meaning. He began to use the sign-talk, slowly and deliberately.

"You should both be ashamed. You dishonor me by fighting in my village."

Both began to relax a little.

"Now put away your weapons."

Cautiously, they did so.

"Traveler, your tribes are enemies of the north?"

Traveler nodded, still keepng a wary eye on Three Owls.

"I am sorry. I suspected, last night. They have been here nearly a moon. I knew they were from your country, but—"

"It is nothing," Traveler signed, calmer now. "I will

not dishonor your hospitality, my chief. But I will trade nothing to him."

"Of course."

The chief turned to Three Owls.

"It will be best," he signed, "if you and your friend leave. You have insulted the family of my guest."

Three Owls stared arrogantly a long time before he sneered and turned to go. He paused to throw an obscene gesture at Traveler and a cruel glance toward Star. Then he stalked away, followed by his companion.

Star felt a mixture of relief and dread. Relief because this scene was over, and dread because she was certain that it was not over. They would encounter this pair again.

She felt exhausted, completely empty. She was still somewhat puzzled over what had happened. Traveler had become livid with rage over the offer to buy her, yet he had done the same thing himself only a few moons ago.

There was a difference. She felt it herself, though she could not define it. Perhaps it dealt with the enmity between the tribes of the two men. She would ask Traveler about it when the incident had had time to cool off, and they resumed their journey north.

Star did not even notice that she was now assuming the resumption of the journey, and her part in it. She had forgotten for the moment her intention to escape.

There was one other thing which distracted her attention and muddled her thoughts. It was to provide more questions, more wonder, and more sleepless nights, before she learned the answer.

The other shocking thing about the confrontation in the village of Hunts-In-The-Rain was this: when Three Owls' knife had come whispering out of its sheath, the girl had been astonished to see that it was a shiny medicine knife, similar to that which Traveler had traded for her.

19

» » »

Winter Bear dipped his paddle rhythmically, trying to match the stroke of his cousin behind him. The canoe slid swiftly upriver. Bear was disappointed that it had been necessary for them to leave so quickly. Their stay in the village of Hunts-In-The-Rain had been pleasant.

If only Three Owls had not become so distracted by the captive girl of the trader's. She was pretty, of course, but there were plenty of other women. Why make such a scene over one?

He sighed. That was the way his cousin did everything, by extremes. People had always said that Three Owls was the brighter, the more intelligent, of the two. Bear had been content with that. He was easily led, had no great ambitions. He knew his strength, was happy in it, and if he was warm and his belly full, why worry about anything else?

When Three Owls had suggested a journey south to see new sights and new country, Winter Bear had agreed. They had been gone for nearly a full year now, and had seen and done much.

But Three Owls had changed. He had become arrogant and demanding. His judgment was not valid any longer. Bear did not know what to do, but he was certain that at some point he, Winter Bear, must begin to make the decisions for the pair.

He was distressed when they had been asked to leave the village where they had wintered. He had made many friends there. But what else could their hosts do?

Three Owls had made improper advances to the wife of a popular young subchief. Even Bear knew that different tribes had different rules about women. Owls should have known better.

And now, he had done it again. Bear had tried to tell him. It did not matter that the trader was a traditional enemy. He was a guest in the village. And to try to buy the woman from an enemy was purely stupid. Even Bear knew that.

His cousin had argued that a confrontation would allow him to kill the trader and take his woman, both. "You can share her, Bear," he said with a leer.

That part sounded good. The girl was very pretty. But the plan was bad. Bear did not have the courage to say so, and the result was disastrous. They had been requested to leave another pleasant village.

While Bear was disappointed and sad, he knew that behind him Three Owls burned with anger. He could tell by the savage strokes of the paddle, the expulsion of tight-drawn breath. Even Bear, with his massive strength, could hardly match the anger-driven pace of his cousin.

He was not certain where the anger was directed. It should be toward Three Owls himself, Bear knew, but it was probably at others. Bear had learned that when his cousin was surly and moody it was not good to question him. Very easily, Three Owls could fly into a rage and strike out at anyone near.

In this case, Bear was the only one near, so he would be vulnerable. The raging anger might be at the trader, or the girl, or even Chief Hunts-In-The-Rain, but the recipient would surely be Winter Bear.

So he said nothing. He had been saved from one important confrontation when they stepped into the canoe. Bear had glanced questioningly at his cousin, ready to argue if the direction chosen did not seem logical. But Three Owls had said nothing. He merely pointed upstream, sat down, and picked up his paddle.

'They were going home. The angry Three Owls could have easily decided on the other direction, or on some other course. Bear had feared that he might want to stay in the area to bring harm to someone, but it seemed not. They were moving swiftly upriver.

That was good. It would take many sleeps, but when they came to their own people, Bear would be glad. Someone else could worry about the raging temper and irrational behavior of his cousin. One thing was certain. He would go on no more journeys with Three Owls.

Finally, as shadows began to lengthen, Three Owls appeared to be tiring. The strokes on the canoe paddle were smoother, more even, the urgent push abandoned. Bear could feel the difference even without turning to look. It was easier for him to match the cadence.

Now he began to look for a place to stop for the night. An open clearing, a treeless area on the bank. The east bank, preferably, across the river from the people they had left.

A gravel bar jutted into the river, and Bear pointed wordlessly. The slim craft responded to the paddles, and they angled to a landing.

Neither spoke until the fire was crackling and they began to relax for the night. The canoe was drawn well up on the gravel bar.

"It will be good to be home," hazarded Bear.

"That will be a long time."

"Yes, but the unpleasantness is behind us."

Three Owls looked sharply at him, making Bear's neck hairs prickle.

"For some, the most unpleasantness is still ahead," sneered Three Owls.

"I do not understand."

"Of course not, Bear. You think slowly. That is why I lead, and not you."

"But what—?"

"Look, cousin," the other explained with exaggerated patience, as to a child, "the trader is traveling north, toward our country. We will wait for him."

"Here?" Bear was dismayed.

"Of course not, stupid one. Farther north, nearer our own country, where he has no friends."

He chuckled to himself, a dry, mirthless little sound.

"They will learn that they cannot insult Three Owls."

The heart of Winter Bear was very heavy. Would his cousin ever understand?

20

》》》

"**P**ut your foot right in the middle," instructed Traveler.

Star grasped the sides of the canoe and gingerly placed a foot in the craft.

"That is right. Over the end, not from the side."

He paused for a moment as the girl moved forward.

"Is it true your people have never seen canoes?"

"Of course," she snapped irritably, distracted from the delicate problem of maintaining her balance, "what would we do with such a thing?"

It was not really a question. There were many things used by the People that would be completely foreign to Traveler's experience, too, she told herself.

She moved forward a step, and the slim canoe tilted precariously.

"In the middle! Stay in the middle!"

Star bent her knees and crouched, holding tightly to the sides, waiting for the shivering tremor to cease. The thing seemed alive. Its spirit would know, she was certain, that she was a land person, and would try to throw her from the boat. Was it not wiggling alarmingly at this very moment?

The canoe steadied, and she took a deep breath, a pause to think. She was really not unskilled in water. She could swim like an otter, as could most of the Rabbit Society, the learning society of her tribe. Children were taught familiarity with water. It was only that this river was so big and so dirty.

And the flimsy shell was so fragile, she feared. It was shallow, slender, and pointed at both ends and seemed so shaky and unstable.

"Go ahead," called Traveler behind her, still holding the stern of the canoe to steady it. "Move to the front."

She looked ahead, the several steps she would have to take to reach the front. It was a long way.

"Could I take the back," Star called over her shoulder, "until I have learned more?"

"No, little one," Traveler laughed. "The experienced one sits in the back. It is guided from the back. You must start with the front."

She looked ahead and took another cautious step. The canoe lurched from side to side, but not as violently as before. She was adjusting to the spirit life of the craft, in spite of herself.

It was really a matter of balance, she now realized. Much like riding a horse. If she could relax, allow her muscles to adjust to the movement of the canoe and the water, yet ready to flex when necessary. Yes, much like adjusting to the motion of a horse.

She had always been a good horsewoman, having ridden since before she could remember. Some of her earliest memories included warm spring afternoons on the back of a dependable old mare. Children were tied safely to the animals' backs as they were turned out to graze. A youngster could doze, rocked by the gentle motion of the horse, or wake and pretend to be a hunter or a warrior. Thus the children of the People could ride well, almost before they could walk.

Pale Star had excelled on horseback, perhaps aided by the fact that her family had always raised the best. Their blood lines reached all the way back to the First

Elk-dog, brought to the People by Star's ancestor, Heads Off. Through the generations, there had been individual horses whose names were legend. Gray Cloud, Gray Cat, even Owl Dung, the odd-colored gelding ridden by Star's grandmother in Running Eagle's War.

There had been the influx of new blood a generation before from the legendary Dream Horse of the northwest country, captured by Star's kinsman Horse Seeker.

"Go ahead," Traveler spoke again behind her, bringing her thoughts back to reality. "Move on up."

More confident now, Star moved forward, balancing by holding lightly to the sides and placing her foot precisely in the center of the canoe with each step. She reached the front and knelt. She felt the craft rock slightly as Traveler stepped in and pushed away from shore. In the space of a heartbeat, they were gliding smoothly across the surface.

She was thrilled at the feeling, much more than she expected. There was a freedom, a release from the restrictions of earth. This must be what the spirit-world is like, she marveled.

Or perhaps this is what an eagle feels as he soars above the prairie. The freedom of motion, freedom to ride the wind.

"Now take your paddle," Traveler was saying. "You must learn to handle the canoe with me, in case Plum Leaf is ill."

Star had only a moment to consider that statement before she felt the paddle that her companion held nudge her shoulder.

"Move slowly," he cautioned.

Carefully, she accepted the paddle and brought it into the position of use. Traveler had instructed her previously how to hold and move the implement. She dipped into the water and the canoe rocked alarmingly.

"No!" called Traveler. "Do not lean to the side. Do it with your arms!"

For some time they maneuvered on the river's surface, learning. Star began to understand what was required.

"You learn quickly, little one," her instructor chuckled. "You will make a good traveler."

She smiled, pleased. It was very simple, really. A matter of balance and timing. If she stroked at the same time as the paddler in the rear, the canoe fairly shot forward. Quickly she learned to anticipate Traveler's stroke and thrust at the same time.

Her arms were becoming tired from the unfamiliar work.

"Let us change sides," Traveler called.

Both swung their paddles over, resting by using different muscles for a while.

"But paddle always on opposite sides," Traveler explained. "That helps the canoe travel straight. The paddler in back chooses which side."

"But, Uncle," Star questioned, "I have seen a canoe with only one man. How does he guide its path?"

Traveler laughed.

"That part will come, little one. It is the shape of the stroke. I will show you later."

Another canoe shot past, and the occupants waved. Star watched the man in the rear closely to see how he directed the craft. Yes, she could see now. It was a matter of the angle of the paddle, and whether it was swept wide away from the side in an arc, or close in and then hooked at the end. She would watch and learn. There might be a time when she would need these skills.

For several days they practiced, Star gaining confidence and skill. Plum Leaf was gaining some strength, though not enough, Star feared.

Traveler seemed pleased with the canoe he had acquired in trade.

"Yes, it moves well, Star. And your skill is improving, too."

He ceremonially painted a pair of large eyes, one on each side of the prow of the craft.

"It is the way of my people," he explained. "In this way it sees the trail ahead."

This was an odd custom, Star thought, but logical.

She well remembered her feelings toward the spirit of the canoe on the first day she stepped into it.

She still thought sometimes of her promise not to escape. Maybe she should speak with Traveler about it. He had a right to know that he need not worry about her leaving the ailing Plum Leaf, that the promise was still good. She would mention it soon.

But that night, Traveler made his announcement.

"Tomorrow," he stated simply, "we start upriver."

21

» » »

The canoe slipped silently over the surface, skimming like the flight of a graceful bird. Star, seated in the front, paused in her rhythmic stroke to point ahead with her paddle.

Traveler answered with a muffled monosyllable and sat quietly, not paddling. The canoe's momentum continued to carry it forward, slowing imperceptibly against the current as it drifted.

On the shore ahead and to the right, a doe lifted her head to watch in curiosity. Water dripped from the dainty muzzle as she stared, ears spread wide.

Behind her there was a silent movement, and a spotted fawn stepped daintily into view, followed by a second.

"It is good," whispered Plum Leaf. "In a year when the deer suckle two, there is food in plenty."

She sat in the center of the canoe, their packs piled around her. There had been very little change in her condition since they had left the village where they had traded. She rested, enjoyed the warmth of the sun on clear days, and shivered against the chill of the wind when it raced along the river. She said little.

There was sometimes a spark of interest in her eyes. A light shone for a moment at a pretty sight, like a sunset or the twin fawns. But mostly Plum Leaf sat, staring ahead upriver, an expression of mute sadness on her tired face.

Star was concerned about the older woman and tried to make things more comfortable for her. The girl was progressively feeling more entrapped in this ongoing situation. Traveler seemed eager to push ahead, to reach his people. She could understand that, the desire to be among his own in time of trouble. Even though, she thought, he will not admit there is trouble.

He still pretended to believe that Plum Leaf was growing stronger and would soon be her old self. His pretended optimism was betrayed by the urgency with which he wished to move upstream to their destination.

Similarly, Traveler had pretended that the instruction of Pale Star in the use of the canoe was really unnecessary. He even went so far as to hint that it was only because of her interest that he bothered to teach her at all. But Star knew. Though Traveler might talk otherwise, she could see that in no way could Plum Leaf carry her share of the task of canoeing up the river.

Star had been quick to learn the skills of the canoe. Within a few days she was able to handle her portion of the task quite well. It required, she realized very early, not strength so much as coordination and rhythm. Traveler had even begun to show her the methods of driving the canoe forward while steering from the rear at the same time.

To her surprise, she found that she enjoyed the thrill of the canoe's motion. As her confidence grew, the enjoyment did also. But, even as her skills expanded, the thought remained that she should talk again to Traveler about her pledge as a captive. It was only that the time had never seemed quite right. She could not have caused him further worry when Plum Leaf lay coughing on her bed of robes inside the lodge.

Actually, it was Traveler himself who had approached

the subject. It was their last night in the village, and
Traveler had announced their departure. Before retir-
ing, however, he drew the girl aside.

"Little sister, I would speak with you."

Star followed him into the darkness a little way.
The man turned and spoke in a voice that was level
yet showed the tightness of worry or concern.

"Long ago," he began, "you gave me a promise that
you would not try to escape."

"Yes, Uncle."

"But you have never taken back that promise. Why?"

"Well, I—"

"Do you wish to do so now?"

This was happening too rapidly, Star felt. There was
much she wished to say to explain her feelings. It
seemed impossible that a few moons ago, she had
come to an uneasy truce with this man because she
saw no other way. Now she felt obliged to explain, as
she would to her father or her uncle, Looks Far, why
she had taken this path of action.

Traveler was talking again.

"I said nothing when we were passing the place
where your trail pointed west. I wondered if you knew."

"Yes," the girl nodded, "I knew. But Plum Leaf was
sick and needed me."

"But she is better now," Traveler insisted.

His voice was tight with emotion.

"If you wished, you could take back your pledge and
escape."

Yes, thought the girl, I could. She could hardly believe this conversation, and how different it was from
their last such talk. No longer was this man her captor, threatening her with death if she attempted escape. Now it was as if he invited her to leave if she
wished. This appeared to be Traveler's promise not to
harm her if she chose such a plan.

Or was this a plea for help? His pride would never
let him say so, but he really needed to know. What
was she planning?

"Uncle," she began slowly, "someday I will return to my people. When I am ready, I will tell you."

Traveler chuckled in the darkness, the most nearly like his old self that he had sounded for some time. He seemed pleased by her answer.

"Fair warning?"

"Of course, Uncle."

"It is good."

"I have not yet learned enough about the use of the canoe. You must teach me more."

He chuckled again, and she knew that he was not deceived. Yet he appreciated the thoughtfulness that spared him pain. Star would not mention the real reason, and it would not be mentioned between them again.

"I will teach you, little one. You will tell me when you have learned enough?"

Now Star laughed.

"You will know. But yes, Uncle, I will tell you before I leave."

She felt better as they turned back toward the lodges. There was the unspoken understanding between them, the knowledge that all was not well with Plum Leaf. Now nothing need be said.

If Star had been able to see the face of her companion in the darkness, she might have seen a tear of gratitude moisten his cheek. But the darkness shielded him as they walked.

"We must sleep," Traveler said almost gruffly. "Tomorrow will be hard work."

22

» » »

It was hard work, more strenuous than it had seemed. Long days of squatting or kneeling in the canoe, muscles aching with every stroke of the paddle. Sometimes it seemed that Traveler, from his position in the rear, would never swing the prow of the craft in to shore for a rest or for night camp. She had been correct about strength. It was not strength that was needed, brute muscle strength, but agility. That and the stamina to continue for long periods without rest.

A goose, startled from the river's edge, rose noisily from the water and flew quickly out of sight. She wondered about the bird for a moment. During the long journeys in spring and fall, did the geese ever feel like this? Did their wings, chest, and shoulders ache from the long flight, until the most important thing in all of life seemed to be to glide down to the water to rest?

She dipped her paddle and stroked again. Behind her in the canoe, Plum Leaf coughed, the dry rattle that had become so familiar. Star felt that it was worsening rapidly, but she dared not say anything to Traveler.

It was now nine, no, ten sleeps they had been on the river. They had come far. Star felt that Traveler seemed pleased with their progress, but he said little. He was withdrawn, as she had come to expect when Plum Leaf's condition worsened.

Several times, they passed the mouths of sizable streams which emptied into the main river. Star assumed that they had names, but Traveler said nothing and she did not ask. She did take notice, for future reference, of some landmarks. A high bluff for some distance along the river, a range of hills in the distance, an island with large trees where they spent a night. She had confidence that she could find her way back downstream and ultimately across the land to her own country.

She watched their direction of travel, trying to keep track of all the twisting and turning of the river's course. At first she was not certain, but a definite feeling kept creeping in. Their direction was changing. She could tell by the angle of Sun Boy's run and the position of the Real-star at night. She said nothing to Traveler for a while. It might be only a curve in the river's course that would correct itself in a day or two. When the new direction continued, she finally accosted Traveler.

"Uncle," she began, "are we changing direction?"

"Some," Traveler grunted.

"I do not understand. Your tribe comes from the Big Waters to the northeast. Plainly, we go northwest."

"Yes, little one. It is easier to go by water. We will have to go by land soon enough."

"We will not reach your people by canoe?"

"No, no, we will leave it, or sell it. We will travel by land again."

Star said nothing but wondered if Plum Leaf would ever be able to travel overland. Even now, they were practically lifting her in and out of the canoe.

"How far?"

"What?"

"How far until we leave the river?"

Traveler merely pointed upstream and grunted. He was in one of his uncommunicative moods. His answer could have been "Tonight" or "Twenty sleeps" or any other distance. A trifle irritated, she rose from the fire.

They had stopped a little early, and there was some daylight left. Well, she would take the opportunity to bathe.

"I go to wash," she said abruptly.

Traveler did not answer. She moved downstream along the shore, looking for the right spot. There had been a sandy beach as they approached the shore. They had, in fact, almost landed there.

Star, at almost the last moment, had seen the jagged tip of a log beneath the surface and called out in alarm. They back-paddled frantically and managed to avoid impaling the fragile canoe.

Now, the girl thought, the same area might be an ideal place to rest and bathe. It was farther than she remembered. Finally she emerged from the bushes on the sandbar. Ah, yes, this was the place. She pulled the buckskin dress over her head, kicked out of her moccasins, and waded into the water.

It was cleaner here than farther downstream and would be pleasant. She swam out into the river, wanting a closer look at the stub which had so nearly destroyed them.

It was a large tree, long dead and waterlogged, with most of the smaller branches broken away. It seemed firmly fastened to the river's bed, probably held in place by the shifting sands around its broken stubs of roots and branches. The water was deeper than her head. She amused herself for a little while by climbing up to stand on the highest of the slippery limbs and diving into the water. It was curious, she thought, that none of the broken branches protruded above the surface. Possibly they had been broken away through the years by other driftwood crashing downstream on some flood's crest. The stub nearest the surface was the most dangerous. It was as thick as her leg, splintered and jagged, and pointing nearly straight downstream.

Star was still studying the corpse of the fallen giant when a motion downstream caught her eye. There, hardly a bow shot away, a canoe rounded a slight curve in the shore and came directly toward her. She sank deeply into the water, trying to make herself inconspicuous, while she decided what to do.

There was no possibility she could avoid being seen, and she could not swim to shore and escape before the canoe was upon her.

Two men were in the canoe, and as it came nearer, the one in the prow noticed the half-submerged head of the girl and pointed. Both paddled furiously and the craft shot forward.

It was time to move. She swam a stroke or two one way, then another, as the steersman deftly maneuvered to head toward the frantic girl.

Finally she screamed and swam straight away from the onrushing canoe. She did not pause until she heard the cry of alarm behind her and only then turned to look.

It was not until now that she recognized the paddler in the front as Three Owls. A frightened chill struck her. She was not certain that she could have carried it off if she had known. She stood, feet barely touching the sandy bottom, and watched.

The cry of warning had come too late. With a ripping crash the jagged stub tore into the canoe's shell, tearing the prow apart. Three Owls was thrown forcibly into the water. The momentum of the craft had carried it forward, sliding down the slanting branch, and now it hung at a crazy angle, stern in the air, while the occupants floundered in the water, trying to recover their floating possessions.

Star swam to shore, knowing the danger was still very real.

"Traveler!" she yelled. "Load the canoe! Hurry! We must leave!"

She paused to slip her feet into her moccasins, and snatched her dress from the grass as she ran.

"Traveler!" she screamed again as she ran. "Can you hear me?"

There was an answering call from their campsite.

"Load the canoe! There is trouble!" she yelled at the top of her lungs.

Star sprinted through the brushy woods, trying to slip into her dress as she ran. Bushes scratched at her body, but she did not notice. She continued to call out, repeating her warning. She was certain that Three Owls had recognized her, and the two men would come searching. Their murderous intent toward Traveler had only been stopped by Hunts-In-The-Rain. Toward herself, she shuddered at the thought and ran harder.

The girl broke through the last fringe of brush and into the clearing. Traveler had wasted no time. The canoe was ready to launch. Only a couple of packs remained by the fire. Traveler was lifting Plum Leaf gently to carry her to the canoe.

"Get the packs," he called.

Star swiftly snatched the packs from the ground and ran ahead. She was standing in the water to steady the canoe by the time Traveler reached the bank with his burden. He carefully deposited the sick woman in the center of the craft, and Star scrambled to her own position.

Traveler pushed away and stepped in. The canoe glided smoothly away from shore. Traveler looked downstream, but the scene of Three Owls' debacle was still out of sight, around the curve of the bank.

Star began to breathe a little easier. Their pursuers could not follow them with a ruptured canoe. She picked up her paddle and began to stroke rhythmically.

"Little sister," came the bewildered voice of Traveler behind her, "will you tell me what is happening?"

23

>> >> >>

Pale Star was silent for the next three strokes of her paddle. Only when she had satisfied herself that they were actually under way could she turn to answer Traveler's question.

"Three Owls!" panted the girl.

She poured forth her story, interrupted occasionally by questions from Traveler. He laughed aloud when she told of her trick to cause their canoe to be destroyed.

"And it did? The log speared their canoe?"

"Yes, Uncle. But I am afraid they will repair it and come after us."

Traveler nodded thoughtfully.

"Yes, they will. But it will take several days to do. We will be traveling those days."

"What does it mean, Uncle? They should have been ahead of us."

Traveler nodded again. His face was grim.

"Yes, little one. It is not good. These men mean us harm. They have waited for us to pass and then followed us. It is good that now we know."

"But what will we do?"

"Nothing, except watch and be prepared to protect ourselves. Travel well, of course."

"You know these men, Uncle?"

"No, but I know their tribe. They are enemies of my people."

"But that is far away!"

"Yes, it should not be so. Even enemies should be friends in strange country."

"I do not understand."

Traveler gave a deep sigh before he answered.

"Nor do I."

But I do, he thought to himself. They hate me, but it is not because I am an enemy. It is because they want you, little one.

"They are very dangerous," he said aloud. "We must take great care."

Star nodded and continued her rhythmic paddling for a while. There was no doubt in her mind what Traveler meant. She could practically feel the enmity and lust that had radiated from the man in the canoe. It was like a puff of chilly air on a warm night.

She remained quiet a little longer, then spoke again.

"What will we do now, Uncle? It will soon be dark."

"Yes. I think we cannot stop, at least on this side of the river."

"There will soon be a moon," observed Plum Leaf. "We could travel."

It was the first time she had spoken since they reembarked. Her voice sounded weak and old in the deepening twilight.

"But you are tired," protested her husband.

"Yes, but afraid, too," Plum Leaf answered. "We must move. I will be all right."

As if to prove her statement, she lay back and curled up in the center of the canoe. It did seem that this would be the best course of action to take.

The tired paddlers continued to work while darkness fell and stars began to appear. A scatter of silver reflected from the river's surface in calmer portions of the water. In the dark woods along the shore, unfamiliar night birds called.

It was almost fully dark when Traveler spoke.

"Look," he pointed.

The canoe was just rounding a long curve in the river's course. An uninterrupted stretch of water lay ahead, bending gently to the northeast. There, rising above the tops of night-black forest, they could see the red arc of the full moon.

"*Aiee!*" said Star softly.

There was much to appreciate in beauty anywhere, she reflected. It was not the same as the rise of the moon over tallgrass prairie, but beautiful nevertheless.

It was useful, too. From one moment to the next, they could see the dark of the river lighten with silvery moonlight. It was pleasant to travel with cool night breezes stirring the damp air.

Plum Leaf had fallen asleep, still curled among the baggage in the bottom of the boat. Star hoped that she was comfortable.

She reflected on the change that she had seen in the older woman since they met a few moons ago. Plum Leaf had been the strong and dynamic companion of her husband. Now she had become as helpless as a child. It startled the girl for a moment as she realized that on the trip down the river last season, the paddler in the front had been Plum Leaf. Now she could scarcely stand without help.

Star had watched her become weaker by the day, less and less able to care for herself. At the present rate, it seemed doubtful that the dying woman would live to reach her husband's people.

And still, thought Star a little irritably, Traveler pretends he thinks her stronger. It might become necessary, she pondered, for her to insist on a serious talk about the sick woman. She would try to start such a conversation. Maybe when they stopped.

The initial excitement had now worn off, and Star was beginning to realize just how tired she actually was. Aching muscles were stiffening again. She would remind herself of the danger behind, and this would give her the impetus to drive ahead a little longer.

She was very glad when Traveler pointed to a sandbar ahead adorned with a few scrubby willows.

"We will stop there."

Star nodded without answer, and the canoe slid smoothly to a stop. Star, proficient by now in this portion of her job, leaped ashore and pulled the prow of the canoe higher up the bank.

Traveler moved forward to rouse the sleeping Plum Leaf, but she lay silent. He picked up some items of baggage and handed them to Star, who carried them ashore.

When she returned, Traveler was just stepping from the canoe with Plum Leaf in his arms. Something was wrong.

"Is she all right, Uncle?"

"Yes," he murmured, sounding numb and wooden. "She has crossed over. She is dead."

Star stood awkwardly, unable to say anything. It was a surprise that was really no surprise at all. What could she say?

Traveler stood there in the bright moonlight, tears glistening on his uplifted face, holding the still body.

The canoe began to drift gently in the current, and Star stepped past the grieving husband to drag it ashore.

She straightened and approached him again.

"I am sorry, Uncle. You knew?"

"Yes," he said quietly. "I have known all along."

24

» » »

They wrapped the frail body in her robe and next morning carried it to a rocky glen high above the river. Traveler scooped out a pocket next to the rock shelf and tenderly tucked Plum Leaf's remains away in it.

They carried stones to cover the grave. Then they sat for a little while, looking around the peaceful scene.

"It looks much like the woodlands of her own country, Uncle."

"Yes, I saw that, too."

"Would it be all right if I sing my people's Mourning Song?"

Tears filled the eyes of Traveler.

"She would like that."

The clear sad wail of the Song of Mourning floated over the brushy glen and along the river. Star was cautious not to sing as loudly as she might have. This was unfamiliar country. It was possible, even, that their pursuers might have come overland to attempt to overtake them.

"Come, little one, we must go."

"Of course, Uncle."

The Mourning Song should be sung for three days, but sometimes it was not possible.

They loaded the canoe in silence and pushed off, after a long look downstream for possible pursuit. Traveler seemed in no hurry, paddling with a leisurely rhythm. Star realized that he was reluctant to leave.

"It is good," he said once, almost to himself.

"What?"

"It is good, that she crossed over on the river. She loved to travel on the river. Did I tell you how good Plum Leaf was with the paddle?"

"No, Uncle. I never saw her use the canoe."

"That is true," he said, as if he was almost astonished at the idea.

They moved in silence for a while longer, and then Star spoke again.

"What now?"

Traveler broke free from his memories and returned to the present again.

"What did you say?"

"I said, what will we do now?"

"Oh."

"Traveler, we must plan. Where are we going?"

"You wish to return to your people?"

"Of course," the girl snapped.

She was irritated at his failure to face reality. Then she softened.

"I am sorry, Uncle, but we must plan. We cannot just travel on the river. I do not know where we are going. Please tell me your plans."

"Of course, little one. Look, let us stop on the sandbar ahead. We will talk."

They pulled ashore and built a small fire of driftwood. It was almost a ritual, the fire. Any serious council at which decisions were to be made required a fire.

"Now," began Traveler, seating himself across the little fire from the girl, "what must we do?"

"Uncle," she suggested, "you have been good to me, but you know that I would wish to return to my people."

He nodded thoughtfully.

Star hesitated to introduce her next idea, but finally blurted it out.

"Would you come with me, to the country of my tribe? You have never been there. You could trade. My father would be proud to thank the man who has helped me."

Traveler pondered a long time.

"I am made to think that this is good," he said finally. "But there are many problems. It is far, and the season is passing."

"But it would be faster down the river."

"Yes, that is true. But we would have to slip past our enemies, and then wonder if they followed us."

The girl had not thought of that. She was unused to the idea of a water trail, a trail that led only upstream or down. It would be impossible to leave the river to go around a potential problem. The dread of another encounter with Three Owls and his companion sent a chill up her spine.

"Look, little sister," said Traveler suddenly, "here is a plan. Let us go on to my people. We can winter there and then in the spring travel to your country."

Star thought about the suggestion.

"How far to your tribe?"

Traveler shrugged.

"Nearly a moon, but closer than yours. We can get goods to trade, pipestone, arrow points, tobacco, and then have better trading with your people."

Star did not fail to notice the use of "we" when Traveler spoke of the trading supplies. Nevertheless, it was a good plan. By the time they could go downstream now, the season would be late. Autumn would bring unreliable weather. Yes, it would be better to plan as Traveler had said.

"It is good, Uncle."

Traveler smiled broadly.

"Good. Then, we go."

"Tell me, first, about our journey. You said we go overland?"

"Yes. Then we come to the lakes, the Big Waters, where my people live."

"You mean, *this* is not the Big Water?"

"No, no," Traveler laughed. "Little one, you cannot even see across the Big Water. We could not cross it in a canoe, even in many sleeps."

"*Aiee!*" murmured Star to herself.

She had not understood. She dimly remembered, now, the legends of how her ancestor, Heads Off, had come to the People from "across the Big Water." But somehow, she had always thought that the stories said from the *south*. It was confusing. Well, she would ask her uncle Looks Far when she saw him next season. Now, for the first time in a long while, she could begin to make plans.

"It is good," she cried, jumping to her feet. "How long until we leave the river?"

Traveler rose and scattered the fire, tossing the larger sticks into the water to quench them.

"Not far. Three, four sleeps."

25

» » »

They sat before spread robes, Traveler haggling with those who came to trade. Star acted as his assistant, smiling at the curious who wandered past, injecting a remark here and there to assist in the transaction. She knew that Traveler felt she was playing her part well.

They had arrived at the village of White Squirrel the previous day. This chief, it appeared, was even a better friend of Traveler than Hunts-In-The-Rain. He welcomed them into his lodge, and the two men spent long in discussion and exchange of news that evening.

White Squirrel and his wives were quite saddened by the news of Plum Leaf's death.

"That one was a strong one, a great woman, my friend," the chief sympathized, while his wives raised a mourning wail.

"Yes, I know. It was hard to let her go."

A tear of sadness moistened Traveler's eye.

"Is this your new wife?" White Squirrel indicated Pale Star.

Again, Star saw a momentary flash of anger on Traveler's face, as there had been once before at such an inference.

"No," he snapped irritably. "This is my daughter."

"Oh."

The chief's answer indicated that he understood, but his expression said plainly that he did not. His confusion was evident. He had known Traveler and Plum Leaf for many years, and knew quite well that they had no daughter. Now Traveler had introduced this attractive young woman as his daughter. He shrugged. It made little difference, he supposed.

Star watched the chief's reaction closely. It was the second time that someone had questioned her relationship with Traveler. She had originally thought of him simply as her captor. Later, he had become a friend, a father figure. She felt very close to him now, more so since they had mourned together over the loss of Plum Leaf. But she had never, at any time, thought of Traveler as a husband. He was more than twice her age. Three times, maybe. Surely he thought of her only as a daughter.

She cast a sidelong glance at Traveler. He still looked angry and uncomfortable over the question his friend had asked in all innocence. His indignation was quite evident.

Nothing more was said, and the subject was not mentioned again.

"You are welcome in my lodge," White Squirrel was saying.

He beckoned them to follow and assisted in carrying part of their packs.

"You have things for trade?"

"Of course. Many things. And we have no use now for the canoe. I will trade it or leave it here until next season, if you will allow."

"If you wish," the chief nodded.

"We will see how the trading goes," Traveler stated absently.

It was at about that moment that a woman walked toward them wrapped in a brilliantly colored robe. Star had never seen such flaming red and yellow. How, she wondered, could such colors be painted on a robe? Where did the paint come from?

She watched closely as the woman paused to speak to the chief. Star saw to her amazement that the color was not painted but was part of the fur itself. She peered more closely.

Then the amazing thing happened. A stray puff of breeze caught the corner of the robe and turned it inside out. Star gasped. There was no skin side to the robe. On both sides was short, soft fur of brilliant color.

"*Aiee!*" she exclaimed. "What animal has fur on both sides of its skin?"

The men laughed.

"You have never seen a blanket, little one?" Traveler asked.

"Blanket?"

"Yes." He took the edge of the robe and showed her the texture. "This is made of just fur, not a skin. You have never seen one?"

"No. Where do they come from? Why do you not have one?"

Traveler laughed.

"I had one but traded it. They are much prized. Maybe you will have one someday."

Star felt the blanket between thumb and forefinger. It seemed soft, warm, and light in weight. It was easy to see why such robes were in great demand.

"Where do they come from?"

"The *Yen-glees* bring them for trade."

"*Yen-glees?*"

"Yes, a tribe from far away. Across the Big Water. They have many things of strong medicine."

"They are hair-faced?"

"Sometimes. Not always. They cut their face hair with knives instead of plucking it."

Star's thoughts whirled. This must be the tribe who brought the shiny medicine knives.

"Knives like the one you traded for me?"

"What? No, no! That was a knife for eating, or

skinning. Even fighting. They use a special knife for face hair. It is used for nothing else."

Aiee, what a strange tribe, thought Star. To use a knife for only one purpose! Again, she wondered if this could be the tribe of her ancestor. Another thought occurred to her.

"Is the knife for cutting face hair made of the same shiny medicine rock?"

"Iron? Yes, they make many things of iron."

"Where does it come from?"

"They dig it from the ground, I am told. How do I know, little one? You ask too many questions."

The woman wearing the blanket walked on.

"My friend," spoke White Squirrel, "how long will you stay?"

Traveler shrugged.

"Three, four sleeps. Until the trading is finished."

"You go to your people?"

"Yes."

"It is good! I will take a party that way soon. You can travel with us for safety."

Traveler nodded agreement.

Star said nothing, but her thoughts were busy. White Squirrel had mentioned safety, yet he knew nothing of the enemies that followed them. This must mean, then, that they were going into a dangerous area.

How strange, the girl thought. A tribe of hair-faces who use medicine knives for many purposes, and make robes from fur with no skin. Could these *Yen-glees* be the danger that Squirrel spoke of? It seemed not. Traveler had not spoken of them as a danger.

What then? It was all very confusing and a little frightening. Well, Traveler would tell her what she needed to know.

26
» » »

There were nine in the party besides Traveler and Pale Star. White Squirrel was the leader.

For the first day's travel they moved in an easy, relaxed manner, without much concern. It was the same sort of travel overland that Star was accustomed to with Traveler and Plum Leaf. The leader called for an occasional rest stop at a source of good water.

The sun was warm but not uncomfortable, and Star found that she was enjoying the day. The gently rolling landscape was a mixture of open meadows and woods. Occasionally they would cross an exposed hilltop and she would have a few moments when she could see for a long way. In the dim blue of distance it was possible to see the earth's rim. Star longed for the open prairies of her people.

On the second day of the journey, there was a noticeable difference in attitude in the party. Travel was slower, more cautious. The main body of the party remained close together, with scouts ahead and on the flanks.

"What is it, Uncle, is there danger?" Star asked.

"Maybe, maybe not," Traveler smiled cheerfully. "But keep your bow ready."

Star was carrying a bow Traveler had obtained for her at the village. She was proficient in its use. The children of the People, both boys and girls, were instructed in the use of weapons at an early age. How long ago, in another world, that now seemed to her, the games and contests that were part of learning in the Rabbit Society.

The land was more wooded now, with occasional open areas. During a halt, a scout returned and conversed seriously with the chief. Star could not understand the language, and they did not use sign-talk, so she was completely without understanding. Still, she knew it was serious by the demeanor of all the men.

"What is it, Traveler? I do not understand."

"There is sign of the enemy," he answered seriously. "We must be ready."

Star was completely frustrated now. She did not understand this sort of conflict. During her lifetime, the People had been basically at peace, allies of their former foes. The stories of old battles told of maneuvering and charges on horseback, the use of lance and ax and sometimes the bow. It had been rare for the People to fight on foot since they had the elk-dog.

Now, here were White Squirrel's warriors, expecting an attack at any time. They were calmly considering it the usual way of things. Men checked their bows, touched their knives to reassure themselves.

"Will there be a fight?" Star asked anxiously.

"Maybe," Traveler shrugged in his irritating noncommittal manner. "We must be ready."

Star's hands were moist and sweaty on the bow. She had never loosed an arrow at anyone. Her largest living target had been a deer. That had been a clean kill, she reminded herself, despite her pounding heart and shaky hands. Yes, if it came to it, she could fight in her own defense.

But nothing happened. All that day and the next,

there was no further sign of any danger. The party began to relax.

It was just before dawn that the attack came. White Squirrel's warriors were beginning to stir and prepare for the day. Star was awake, sleepily watching the start of the day's activity and hating to leave the warmth of her robe.

She could see a sentry posted inconspicuously against the trunk of a large tree near the clearing.

A warrior crawled from his robe, stretched and yawned, and walked a few steps into the woods to empty his bladder. Then he suddenly gave a warning yell and sprinted back toward the camp, dodging and twisting as he ran. In the growing light, Star caught a glimpse of an arrow which reached out after him and missed, shattering against a tree.

Then the air was full of yells and screams and the buzzing of arrows like angry wasps. Star fitted an arrow to her bowstring and crouched, searching for a target. She could see only flitting forms among the trees. She dared not shoot for fear of hitting one of their own party by mistake.

There was a noise to her right, and she whirled to face a charging warrior with a wicked-looking ax upraised. Before she could release her arrow, the man was struck backward and fell heavily, grasping at an arrow in his flank. One of White Squirrel's warriors leaped forward, and his ax swung quickly.

It was all over in the space of a few heartbeats, it seemed, and the enemy was gone, leaving two dead behind. Of White Squirrel's party, one had a deep slash across his shoulder and chest. Another had an arrow sticking through the fleshy part of his upper arm.

Men were talking, laughing, and beginning to recount individual experiences as the moment of excitement subsided.

Star stood numbly. She had not even loosed a single arrow in the short, intense skirmish. Was this how a battle happens? Her mind was full of questions, but she was unable to form any of them into words.

A warrior stooped over the dead man in the woods and drew his knife. He grasped the fallen enemy's hair and circled the top of the head with quick slashes, ripping free a bloody trophy. He returned to the camp, holding it aloft.

Star was horrified. She had never heard of such a custom.

"What is it, little one?" Traveler spoke at her elbow. "Are you all right?"

"What? Oh, yes, Uncle. And you?"

"Of course. You look sick."

She pointed, fascinated, to the warrior with the handful of bloody hair.

"He skinned the hair."

"Of course. He took the scalp of the man he killed."

"But why?"

Traveler stared at her in astonishment. Then a light of understanding dawned.

"Ah, yes. Your people do not take scalps?"

"Of course not. Why would we do such a thing?"

"Ah, little one, you have much to learn."

Her anger boiled as the stress of the morning found relief.

"How am I to learn," she fumed, "when you tell me nothing? And stop calling me 'little one'!"

Traveler stared at her, wide-eyed, as if he had never seen her before. He started to laugh, then thought better of it, and became serious.

"You are right."

There was a pause, as if he had started to say "little one" again, and decided against it.

"Come, sit," he motioned. "You are right. You are a grown woman, and there are things you need to know."

27
» » »

During the next few days, as they traveled, Star learned much about the strange new country and its people. Traveler talked to her at each stop.

"There are tribes here who have always been enemies," he had begun, after the skirmish. "They kill each other when they can."

"Your tribe?"

"Well, yes. But mine is small. We are not great fighters but traders. Still"—he spread his palms in frustration—"some call us enemies."

"Three Owls' tribe?"

"Yes, that is one. We have friends, too, like White Squirrel's people."

"It is much the same in my country," she agreed, "but—"

"Let me go on, lit—uh, Star. There came to our country the *Yen-glees* from far away across the Big Water."

"Yes. From the north?"

"No, no."

"But the Big Water is north."

"No, this is another Big Water."

He paused in consternation.

"You know nothing, girl!"

"And you know nothing of my country," she snapped.

"Yes, of course. Look, Star, the Big Waters where we go now are lakes. Fresh water. The one we will see first is called *Mishi-ghan.* The *Yen-glees* come from across another Big Water, far to the east of here. It tastes of salt."

"*Aiee!* Salt?"

"Yes."

"There are salty springs sometimes in my country."

"No, no, the whole Big Water is salty. Now do not interrupt. Where was I?"

"The *Yen-glees.*"

"Oh, yes. They came and built lodges and towns. They trade for furs. Some of them plant."

"Growers?"

"Yes, like growers. And they bring many warriors."

She nodded.

"Then there is another tribe from across the Big Water—the salty one."

"Another? There are two hair-faced tribes?"

"Yes. They are the *Fran-coy.* They are enemies of the *Yen-glees* where they come from."

"So they fight here?"

"Yes. The *Fran-coy* bring many soldiers, too, but neither has enough to kill the other."

"So?"

"So," he picked up a stick and drew a line in the dirt, "the *Yen-glees* are south of this, and the *Fran-coy* to the north."

"And where is this line?"

"It is nowhere!" he exploded in frustration. "Look, there is not a line. Only that one tribe is usually north of the other."

"But what does that have to do with this morning?"

"Nothing! But look, we must travel now. I will tell you more later."

They rose to begin the day's travel.

Star's head was filled with thoughts as they walked. *Two* hair-faced tribes of outsiders! She wondered which was the tribe of her ancestor, Heads Off. Or, even stranger, his might have been yet another! And she still did not understand how this all related to the events of the morning.

By the first stop, she was bursting with curiosity.

"Traveler, tell me more."

"Yes. Well, the *Yen-glees* and the *Fran-coy* are enemies."

"Yes, you told me that."

"Both are pushing west, and neither is strong enough to kill the other. So they get their friends to help them."

"Their friends?"

"Yes, the tribes in the area. One tribe is loyal to the *Yen-glees*, another to the *Fran-coy*."

"And the tribes kill each other because of these outsiders?"

"Well, yes, but they were enemies before. They have always been. Now they are given gifts for doing what they have always done anyway."

He chuckled at the thought.

"Gifts?"

"Yes. Knives of iron, blankets, other things."

"But I still do not understand. What has this to do with this morning?"

"Oh, yes, the scalps. Well, if someone is to be rewarded for killing enemies, he must have proof, yes? The scalp is proof of a dead enemy."

Star shuddered. Then another thought came to her.

"They are rewarded by the number of scalps they bring? That is no proof. They could be anyone's hair!"

"Yes," he agreed sadly. "Some sell scalps to both sides."

"Which side started this, Uncle?"

"No one knows now. People take scalps more to show their manhood now, anyway."

"Which side are your friends?"

"I would like to trade with both," Traveler said

earnestly. "There is more trade that way. So I try to stay friends with both by killing neither. Sometimes it is hard."

"Which side do White Squirrel's people fight for?"

"I am not sure," Traveler pondered. "Neither *Francoy* nor *Yen-glees* have come this far west yet. They probably have not decided."

"But, Uncle, they take scalps!"

"Yes, but that is something else now. It does not matter which side to many. Scalps are a thing of value, like furs, and prove manhood. Some who take scalps here do not even know how it started."

The party was preparing to resume travel now. Star shuddered again as she picked up her pack. She had learned many things today, some of them very alarming.

The two tribes of outsiders, bringing gifts but rewarding anyone for killing. Their medicine knives, and the bright blankets they brought. She would be pleased to own a blanket but was repulsed at the idea of trading scalps for it. She wondered how many scalps it would take and then hated herself for wondering such a thing.

She shook her head in disbelief. It would be easy, she realized, to slip into the way of thinking that these people found natural.

Another emotion came crowding into her head, tightening her throat. It was fear. Never, since she was first captured, had there been this vague uneasiness. It was an ill-defined fear, a dread, different from the physical fear she had felt in Three Owls' presence.

It seemed terrible to her that almost anyone in this forbidding land might kill a stranger, just to take his hair.

It was a land where everyone seemed to have gone mad. How could anyone defend himself in such a world gone mad?

It was no wonder that Traveler preferred to spend long periods of time far away. Star was already looking forward to next spring, when they could leave to return to her own people.

28

>> >> >>

Despite the ominous character of the things Star had learned from Traveler, the days were uneventful. They traveled, ate, slept, and paused for rest.

Occasionally she asked further questions, attempting to learn more of the customs of the region. The dread and fear she had felt initially was still there but somewhat less urgent now.

It was easy to forget the conflicts, the political turmoil, the murder and scalping, in the beauty of each day. The sunlight of early autumn and the smells of ripening made travel pleasant. The country was, for Star, not as attractive as her prairie, but she found it beautiful, too, in its own way.

Several times there was a period of alarm. The scouts would quietly hurry back to the main party, converse with White Squirrel, and just as quietly melt into the shadows of the woods again. The party would stop, always in a good defensive position, post lookouts, and wait. Eventually the scouts would come back and give the signal, and travel would resume.

They encountered no more of the enemy. In fact,

after a few days, the entire party appeared to become more relaxed. The continuous vigilance softened a trifle.

Star was confused about this. It was almost as if the threat was past. She inquired about it.

"Traveler, is the danger over?"

"What?"

"Is the threat of the enemy gone?"

"Oh. Some, yes. We have passed through the country of White Squirrel's enemies, so it is better here. But we are closer to a *Fran-coy* fort, too."

"This removes danger?"

"Sometimes. It is like when we were with Hunts-In-The-Rain. Enemies who are guests in another's territory do not fight. There is a truce."

Of course. She had not thought of that. Naturally, no enemies of the *Fran-coy* would enter their territory except by stealth. There would be many, however, who would come to trade, yet without a commitment as allies. Among these would be some who were sworn enemies of each other.

It was, perhaps, like the villages of the Growers in her own country. The Growers traded with all, and by common custom, even enemies respected their neutrality.

Only in this way could their function as growers and traders of corn and vegetables be continued. Yes, thought Star, it must be that way with the *Fran-coy*. She, too, began to relax a little.

Several times the party encountered travelers who were apparently friendly. At any rate, they paused to visit with White Squirrel, usually in strange tongues, sometimes accompanied by sign-talk. The talk, it appeared, was mostly of the weather, the scarcity of game, and news of the shifting power struggle between the two groups of outsiders.

"Things are quiet now," one party told them. "The value of scalps is low this season."

Their leader shrugged in resignation.

"Maybe it will be better next year."

Again, Star experienced the chill dread, the prickling of the hairs on the back of her neck. Human lives had become an item for trade for these people, like buffalo robes or dried meat.

One evening as they camped, White Squirrel approached Traveler.

"Tomorrow we part," he stated, using sign so that Star could also understand.

Traveler nodded.

"We thank you for your kindness. It has been good to be with your people, my chief."

"You are welcome in my lodge, my friend. Your canoe will be safe with us until you return."

Traveler nodded again.

"We will come in the spring."

The chief smiled at Star.

"It is good to know you also, little sister. Take good care of my friend Traveler."

There may have been a slight question in his mind, but his dignity had not allowed him more. Since their initial meeting, nothing had been said as to the girl's status and her relationship to Traveler. Star found herself liking this man. Perhaps when they met again there would be opportunity to tell him the rest of her story.

White Squirrel and his warriors left them the next morning, taking a fork of the path which pointed northeast. The last man paused and waved before he disappeared, and the forest closed around him. Traveler and Star picked up their packs and took the trail.

They talked little and covered much distance. Traveler took the lead, and though he was watchful and cautious, Star could feel his growing confidence. This was his country.

"How far to your people?" she asked during a rest stop.

"Three, four sleeps," he smiled.

She had not seen him so relaxed since before the illness of Plum Leaf. Traveler was going home.

"You will find it good to see them," she suggested. "You have parents?"

"No. They are dead. A sister. We will stay with her."

"She has a husband and children?"

"Yes," he smiled. "You will like her family."

As they camped that evening, their hearts were good. Star saw and felt the happiness and relaxation of her companion, and this made her feel good, also.

Their camp site, she felt, could have been more to her liking. Star was still having a little difficulty with the closed-in feeling of the woods. She would have preferred, for instance, an open grassy slope they had passed earlier. This was a small clearing in a timbered area.

It had obviously been used as a camping spot before. There were ashes and burned sticks of other fires. Probably it was one of the traditional camp sites of the region, she told herself, because of the clear spring in the hillside. It was much the same in the prairie. A good spring might have been used by travelers for many generations.

There was always one problem at such a site. Available fuel was scarce, since it was sought by every passing party of travelers. They assembled a few sticks, and Traveler kindled a fire with the fire sticks in his pouch.

"Did you know," he asked over his shoulder, "that my people sometimes start fire with a stone?"

He was teasing, of course, thought the girl.

"Of course, Uncle," she laughed.

"No, really. You have seen sparks from the flint when struck together. It is the same."

"But those will not start fire."

"When struck against a piece of iron," he insisted, "what you called the medicine stone."

"It will start fire?"

"Yes," he nodded.

He was so serious that she was forced to believe him. *Aiee,* what else could this shiny substance do?

"Will you show me?"

"Of course. When we get to my people."

He rose and turned away.

"You feed the fire. I will bring more wood."

Star knelt before the little blaze, feeding sticks expertly to the flame as it grew. Her supply was limited, and she was glad when she heard Traveler's returning steps.

"Good," she said over her shoulder. "I need more sticks."

She turned, extending her hand to receive the fuel, and stopped short. The footsteps she had heard behind her were not those of Traveler. The man standing there in the gathering shadows of the forest was Three Owls.

29

>> >> >>

$\mathbf{T}$ he girl reacted instantly, whirling up from her crouching position with a burning brand in her hand. She had picked up a not quite dry enough branch while waiting for Traveler to return and had laid its leafy end on the fire. The brief thought crossed her mind that it had been stupid to produce so much smoke that way.

But now it proved useful. She thrust the smoldering stick straight at the face of Three Owls. The man tried to dodge, caught the searing brand across his left cheek and ear, and cried out in pain.

"Traveler!" screamed the girl. "Look out! They are here!"

She threw her stick at Three Owls' face and jumped over the fire to run, still yelling her warning at the top of her lungs. She headed back down the trail the way they had come. She knew that direction, while other paths were still unfamiliar to her.

Darkness was deepening, and she was only a few strides into the trees when her path was blocked by Winter Bear. She tried to dodge aside but was knocked down by a sweep of the man's arm. He was on her in an instant, moving quickly for a big man. He grasped her wrist, twisted her to the ground, and sat astride her.

Star fumbled for her waist knife, but barely had the weapon in her hand when the big man knocked it aside. He struck her sharply across the head a time or two, using the front and back of his pawlike hand. Her head reeled.

Three Owls rushed over, yelling at her in rage. For a moment, she thought he would kill her in his fury, but then he quieted. He produced a rawhide cord and looped it around her throat, jerking it cruelly tight. Her breath came in wheezing gasps, and Winter Bear said something to his cousin, pointing to the cord. Three Owls snapped an angry reply but loosed it slightly. She could not understand their tongue but had no difficulty with the meaning of that exchange.

Winter Bear rose and motioned the girl to her feet. She moved to get up, reminded to move slowly by Three Owls' threatening jerk on the cord around her neck.

Star realized that Traveler was probably dead, but she was not ready to admit it.

"Traveler! Be careful!" she yelled.

Three Owls cuffed her sharply across the ear. She would be very cautious and observe for a little, she decided.

The men pushed her roughly back toward the fire. Three Owls, whose face was beginning to blister, tied the rawhide cord to a sapling. It was short enough so that she could not reach the knot behind her easily. He had also forced her to sit, and she could not rise while tied in this position.

Winter Bear returned with an armful of sticks, and the fire grew, lighting the clearing. She tried to evaluate her situation.

The two seemed not to fear the return of Traveler, which argued that he was dead. Still, something told her otherwise. She must be very observant and very careful.

She tried to act defeated, downcast, which was not difficult. She cried, struggled a little, and hung her head while she watched the two closely. They were rummaging through Traveler's packs, dumping the contents on the ground, exclaiming in pleasure over their findings.

Then a realization struck her.

"Ho!" she called to attract their attention. Then she turned to sign-talk.

"Traveler will kill you for this."

Both men laughed.

"Traveler will kill no one. He is dead," signed Three Owls.

"Then where is his scalp?"

The two looked at each other. Three Owls snapped an angry question at his cousin. The other man spread his hands in bewildered protest, obviously explaining to the other. For a moment it appeared that Three Owls would strike him. Then he settled his anger a moment and turned back to the girl.

"Winter Bear killed him," he signed. "He fell from the bluff, and his scalp was not worth going after."

Her heart sank. This she could now believe. Despite the disagreement between the two, and the fact that the slow-witted Winter Bear had bungled his assignment, it appeared that Traveler was really dead. Tears came freely now.

She lifted her head and began to sing, the mournful, rising and falling wail of the Mourning Song of the People.

Three Owls glanced at her irritably, stepped over and slapped her, and silenced her with a thong tied through her mouth and behind her neck. He tied her hands behind her and returned to his plundering.

It seemed a long time before the two settled before the fire and ate, a large meal of dried meat from the supplies of Traveler's packs. They offered the girl none.

She watched them, crying quietly in her grief. She could not have eaten anyway.

Finally Three Owls rose, walked to the spring, and drank. He walked back to the fire, wiping water from his chin, and stared at the girl for a moment. He belched loudly.

Then he unrolled and spread a sleeping robe on a level spot and returned to the tree where Star was fettered. He untied the thong from the tree and pulled her to her feet, pushing her forward. He threw her roughly to the robe, hands still tied, and stood over her a moment.

The firelight flickered on the tight, shiny surface of his blistered cheek and ear, making his cruel leer seem even uglier.

"Now," he told her in sign-talk, "it is time for you to warm my bed."

30
» » »

The next few days were a prolonged nightmare for the girl. She was beaten, repeatedly raped by one or the other of the men, and forced to carry a heavier pack than before. If she stumbled or protested her treatment, she was beaten again.

She decided that the best course was to be as cooperative as possible. That way she endured less pain, fewer beatings, and there was less chance of serious injury. She must save her strength, she told herself. Sometime her opportunity would come, and she must be ready.

Star watched the men carefully, seeking any small thing that would help her when the time came.

Winter Bear was big, sleepy-looking, and strong as a bull. He looked every bit like his name. Star could see how the name came to be. He certainly resembled the grumpy, half-asleep bear, denned for the season in his layers of winter fat. He also appeared a bit simple-minded, though maybe it was only because Three Owls treated him that way. She had to admit that Winter Bear, though rough and clumsy, was better to be with than his cousin.

Three Owls was quick and angry and seemed to enjoy causing pain. He was unpredictable and flighty, too. Sometimes he would smile in an almost friendly manner. Then, when she thought it prudent to smile in return, his anger would flare and he would strike her again. There was nothing she could do that pleased him.

His pleasure in inflicting pain was not limited to his captive. Star watched in horrified fascination one evening while he quietly touched the glowing tip of a stick from the fire to his cousin's bare ankle. Winter Bear roared in pain, and Three Owls laughed with delight. Star had wanted to warn the big man but was afraid of the wrath of Three Owls.

She did not fail to notice the black look of resentment on the face of Winter Bear. Perhaps this was something she could use. Maybe she could come between the two and find ways to fan the flame of discontent she plainly saw on the big man's face. But she must be careful. She realized that Three Owls was near the edge of madness. If he suspected what she was doing, he might easily kill or maim her in a sudden rage.

So she smiled at Winter Bear sometimes, but only when Three Owls was not present. She hoped to make Bear feel that he was her friend. Then, perhaps, in an emergency, he would come to her aid. It was not a good plan, but Star had very little choice.

She still clung to the idea that sometime Three Owls would become careless and she would be able to acquire a weapon of some sort. So far, it seemed unlikely.

She had been beaten once merely for looking at his knife. She was fascinated by it. The weapon was carried sheathed at his waist, but she could see that it was the same one with which he had threatened Traveler. It was of the shiny medicine rock that Traveler had called "iron." She longed to hold the knife, to feel its strength. She was certain that its medicine would work in her favor. How appropriate, she thought, if she could somehow bring vengeance to Three Owls with his own medicine knife.

Star spent little time, however, in fantasy. She was too serious about her goals to waste her thoughts in idle wishing. Her major goal was to escape. The secondary goal must be to kill Three Owls in the process. Otherwise, he was sure to follow her, and she could not spend her lifetime looking over her shoulder in dread. Yes, the more she thought, the more she realized that the two goals were one. It would do no good to escape while Three Owls lived. Likewise, if he was dead, she must escape from Winter Bear, too.

They had changed directions slightly as they traveled, now moving in a more northerly course. She wondered where they were going. The two communicated very little, even between themselves. To Star, they did not bother to converse at all, except for an occasional demand. These were by hand-sign.

Once, when Three Owls had stepped out of the clearing where they camped, Star tried to question Winter Bear.

"Where are we going?" she signed.

Bear blinked stupidly, stared at her, and gave a guttural grunt. Nothing more. She repeated the hand-sign, but the man only turned away. Well, she would try again later.

At least they offered her food now. They had plundered Traveler's supplies to replenish their own, so they now had plenty. Too much, Star thought sometimes, as she once more shouldered a heavy pack. Three Owls still made his cousin and his captive carry the major part of the load.

By now, of course, the carrying of packs was familiar to the girl. She had been with Traveler and Plum Leaf for many moons and had learned the tricks of weight and balance. Her muscles were hard, and she tolerated the rigors of the trail. The constant abuse could easily have killed her otherwise.

Star knew that she must maintain her health. If she became ill, she knew that Three Owls would consider her useless and discard her. There was little chance that he would merely abandon her. He would kill her. It was with more than a little dread that she realized this. If she became useless, a man like Three Owls would try to salvage what he could. If he could not sell or trade her, he would get whatever was possible for her scalp. When she became exhausted, this thought spurred her on a little longer.

Once again, she tried to communicate with Winter Bear. She smiled at him one evening, and then made sign-talk again.

"Where are we going?"

At first she thought he would ignore her again, but then he cleared his throat and made an almost casual hand-sign.

"You will see."

At that moment, Three Owls returned to the camp with a handful of sticks for the fire. He saw the sign, and became illogically furious. He shouted at Winter Bear and stepped across the clearing to strike the girl.

Star cowered and cried out. She had learned that this was the action most desired by Three Owls. He struck her, then stepped back to his cousin, yelling angrily. To her amazement, he slapped Winter Bear full in the face.

Star gasped in astonishment. Among the People, to strike another except in combat was unheard of. It was the greatest of insults.

Bear recoiled slowly and said nothing, but his face burned with shame and anger. Star watched him closely. Yes, the friction between the two was growing. She would try to use it.

Later that evening, she found a brief opportunity to make a sign to Winter Bear.

"I am sorry."

Winter Bear glowered and said nothing but she could see that he understood.

31

》 》 》

Winter Bear sat in the gathering darkness and glared at his cousin across the fire. Now he was convinced that Three Owls was quite mad, but he did not know what he could do about it.

Owls had become more and more irrational. It had begun when they had been asked to leave the village far down the Big River. Maybe even before that, he thought now.

But since the incident of the quarrel over the girl, Three Owls had been worse. His behavior was completely inappropriate, driven by the unreasonable desire to possess this one woman. How stupid, Winter Bear had thought. This one was pretty, yes, but there are many women. Why not find women who would prove less of a risk to acquire? Even he, Winter Bear, could see that.

Still, the possession of this girl of Traveler's seemed the only thing in the world of importance to his cousin. Three Owls had subjected them to cold, hunger, and unnecessary danger to pursue the trail of Traveler.

Bear had thought that his cousin's anger might destroy them both when the canoe was wrecked. Three Owls, in the prow, should have been watching for snags in the river. Instead, he was intent on capturing the girl in the water. Owls never had admitted his fault. He only raved and shouted far into the night about the loss of their supplies.

Winter Bear kept silence. As long as the object of his cousin's wrath was the girl, it would not be directed toward Bear.

They repaired the canoe and hurried after their quarry, Three Owls becoming more and more irrational as they traveled. Winter Bear thought, when they arrived at the village of White Squirrel, that Three Owls would burst with anger. They asked casually about Traveler, who was well known in the area, only to find that he and the girl had already gone. Worse, they were traveling in the protection of the chief and his party.

Three Owls, irrational though he might be, was cunning and clever. He insisted that they leave immediately to try to overtake the party. Then they followed along until Traveler and the girl separated from the rest and they could move in.

Winter Bear was sorry now that he had helped his cousin in this plan. Bear had thought that possession of the girl might somehow bring his cousin to his senses, but it had made him worse. Owls had been furious over the loss of Traveler's scalp, even. A small thing. How was Bear to know that when he struck the man he would throw himself over the bluff?

The girl, trouble though she had been, could not fail to impress a man. She did not complain, she did as she was told. Winter Bear felt a great deal of sympathy as he saw his cousin deliberately hurt the girl for his own pleasure.

Owls had always been like that, hurting people for a joke. Bear gingerly rubbed the still tender blister on his ankle.

The girl had tried to be nice to him, to ask reasonable, friendly questions, and Bear had refused to answer. He was afraid. Yes, for himself as well as for the girl. Three Owls could suddenly rise up in an illogical fury and kill the girl. That would be too bad, because she was warm and soft. Bear wished sometimes that she were his alone.

But he was also afraid for himself. If Three Owls kept behaving as he was now, Bear felt that he might become dangerous even to Bear, his cousin. This had been reinforced this evening, when Owls had slapped them both just for communicating in sign-talk.

It was this inconsistency that bothered Bear. Three Owls did not hesitate to have the captive share the bed of Winter Bear, but he was wild with rage when they tried to communicate.

Yes, clearly the man was mad. After all the years of growing up together, Winter Bear saw that the thing was coming to a climax. He had tolerated the sadistic little tricks, like the red-hot stick on his ankle, all his life. That had merely been part of his cousin's way.

Now it was different. Perhaps it was different, admitted Winter Bear to himself, because of the girl, what was her name? Pale Star, someone had said. The girl had treated him better than Three Owls had, when he came to think of it. Bear was beginning to respect the girl. It hurt him greatly to see Three Owls mistreat her. He did not think he could stand to watch his cousin beat the girl for no good reason.

Yes, he would have to be prepared to do something. When the time came, he would know. He, Winter Bear, would stand in the girl's defense. He would defy his cousin and prevent him from injuring her. Then the girl would respect and admire him.

One thing about this fantasy bothered him. What if Three Owls did not back down? What if he persisted in hurting the girl? He might attempt to kill her, just *because* Bear tried to prevent her abuse.

He thought about it a long time, after the fire had died and Three Owls had ordered the reluctant girl to his bed. Finally, he decided what he must do. The next time his cousin began to abuse her unreasonably, Bear would demand that he stop. Then he must be prepared for the worst. Three Owls would probably not stop, and Bear must be prepared to enforce his demand.

Failing this, there would be only one thing to do to ensure the safety of the girl as well as his own. He must be ready to fight Three Owls.

32

» » »

Star stumbled along the path, exhausted and staggering. She must keep up. Ahead of her strode Three Owls, walking fast enough that she seemed always to be hurrying. She dreaded any mishap that would make her fall behind a few steps, because Three Owls would come back to beat her if she caused a problem.

Behind her on the trail shuffled the stolid Winter Bear. She was no longer afraid of him. In fact, since the incident last night, when Three Owls had struck them both, she had almost felt that she and Winter Bear were conspirators. There was something about the expression on Bear's face that said so. There was a new light, somehow, in the flat-lidded eyes. Star could not have described it or told how she knew, but it was there. A change of some sort. She had had no more opportunity to think about it, beause it was time to take to the trail.

Travel started much like any other day's travel at first, except that the wind was chill. Low clouds obscured the sun, and damp seemed to penetrate to the bone.

Soon the path was becoming damp and slippery from the heavy droplets in the air. It did not seem to be actually raining, but objects exposed to the foggy mist soon became wet. Star labored to maintain footing even on a gentle slope. She could see that Three Owls, walking ahead, was having problems, too.

Her pack made the center of balance too high, and the slippery footing was becoming worse. She paused to shift the load. She wished for a stick to use for balance but could not stop now to find one. Three Owls would be angry.

Behind her, she could hear Winter Bear's occasional grunts as he, too, negotiated the slick path. She turned to glance at him and took a misstep. A smooth stone projected just a trifle above the level of the path, and her foot slid across the moist surface. The unexpected shift in her weight was enough to throw her completely off balance.

Star fell heavily, the pack striking a small tree as she desperately tried to regain her footing. The top-heavy load twisted, and the girl fell on her left side, knocking the breath from her lungs.

She struggled to rise. The twisted pack impeded her, and her struggles opened one of its ties. Part of their food supplies began to spill out on the wet ground. Frantically, she attempted to shrug her shoulders out of the carrying straps.

Three Owls turned and looked back, attracted by the sounds of the struggle. She watched him turn and stride back toward her, anger showing in his face. She struggled harder. She must free her arms to defend her face when the blows came.

The man had nearly reached her when there was a sound behind her and Winter Bear moved forward. He stepped directly over the girl to stand in the path. The growl that issued from his throat was more animal than human.

Star could not understand the words as they shouted at each other, but the meaning was clear. Bear had come to her defense, demanding that his cousin stop.

Three Owls shouted back at the big man and moved forward again.

Bear held up a heavy paw in an unmistakable denial, and Three Owls paused. He looked at his cousin as if he had never seen him before. Once more he shouted and gestured to move aside, but Winter Bear stood fast.

Then Three Owls straightened. Methodically, he took his light belt ax from his waist, and his right arm swung quickly in a full arc. The shiny blade whirled over once, twice, as it flew the few steps that separated the men. It struck Winter Bear in the face with a sickening thud. He fell backward without a sound, to lie staring through the tree tops at the gray sky with eyes that could no longer see.

Three Owls hurried forward, pausing only a moment to glance at his cousin's body. He retrieved his ax and moved toward the girl.

Star had wriggled free of her packs and stood to meet the threat. The man balanced his weapon, ready to throw again. She had never seen the use of the throwing ax before. Star realized it was no use to run. If he could not catch her, he would throw again, and she had seen the deadly results.

"Stop!" she held up a hand in sign-talk.

Three Owls stood, taken aback by her demand. The girl had never stood up to him before. He still held the ax ready.

"I am of no use to you dead," the girl signed. "I can only be useful if I am alive."

It seemed a long time that Three Owls pondered. Then he stopped, methodically wiped the ax clean on Winter Bear's leggings, and returned it to his waist. Now with both hands free, he began sign-talk.

"You will do as I say?"

"Yes," the frightened girl nodded.

"Pick up the pack."

He stepped over Winter Bear's body and down the trail to the packs Bear had dropped. He brought them back, threw them to the ground irritably, and began to sort contents.

Now, Star realized, Three Owls would have to carry more of the load. This bothered him more than the death of Winter Bear.

He rose, shoved a pack toward her, and shouldered one himself. Then he paused, looking over the supplies they were being forced to abandon.

Star lifted her pack to her shoulders, staring at the dead man. She was still terrified, half suspecting that Three Owls would even now turn to strike her down.

He started ahead on the trail but paused and came back.

"Go ahead," he motioned, then "No, wait."

He knelt over Winter Bear's body and drew his knife. Star watched in fascinated horror while Three Owls calmly removed his cousin's scalp and tucked it under the thong around his waist.

33

» » »

P ale Star moved along the trail, trying desperately
to keep ahead of Three Owls. She was terrified that if
she displeased him he would kill her, too. She could
still not believe the calmness with which the man
had killed his own kinsman and then taken his scalp.
Terror made her legs move, kept her feet on the slippery path.

By midday they were meeting occasional other travelers. It was apparent that they were approaching a
sizable village. Star had no idea what sort of people
would be there. Actually, she did not care. Her entire
situation was so hopeless that she only wanted to sit
down and cry.

She wished for a moment to stop, to be alone, to
think. She could see in her mind the still form of
Winter Bear, lying on his back in the trail, with sight-
less eyes staring up at the sky. Someone should mourn
for him. His kinsman, who should have done so, was
his killer. Star would have mourned for him herself
but was afraid of the madness of Three Owls.

One thing was becoming obvious to her. She must

soon find a way to kill Three Owls, before he did so to her. His half-crazed mind could snap at any time. If, she reminded herself, it had not already done so.

Then she would recoil from the idea. That would leave her alone, far from home, in a country where she did not even speak any of the languages. Even being alone, on the other hand, would be better than being with Three Owls.

She had no idea what the penalties for murder might be among Three Owls' people. If, of course, these were his people. She would probably never be believed if she managed to tell the circumstances of Winter Bear's death. Her concern was for what would be done with her when she killed Three Owls.

It made no difference, she decided. It could be no worse than her present status. She must simply choose the best moment for her purpose. Yes, she would watch and wait and see this village and its people.

Three Owls seemed relaxed, at least for him. By this, Star assumed that this was a village where he had visited before, if not his own tribe. People on the trail nodded in greeting, although she thought not in recognition.

She began to notice their dress and their weapons. She saw, to her amazement, that many of the men they met wore shiny medicine knives at their waists. Most of them also carried throwing axes of the same material. So in this region, she realized, the iron medicine rock was almost commonplace.

The other startling thing she noticed was that many people wore blankets. These, too, were almost a common garment.

Star remembered now, Traveler had said that both the tribes of long-haired outsiders wanted many furs and traded these things to get them. Beaver furs were in special demand.

Why, she had asked him, did he not trade for furs? Traveler had chuckled. Sometimes he did, he reminded her, but he usually retraded them. Furs were heavy and bulky, while smaller, more valuable items were more easily carried. He preferred arrow points, beads, knives, and tobacco.

"If I stayed in one place, I would trade in furs, little one," he had told her.

It was strange, how she found herself thinking of Traveler now. She would have loved to have him with her to show her all the new sights and customs of this region. Instead, she found herself a captive, a slave-wife of the madman behind her.

The forest was thinning now, and she saw stumps of many trees which had been cut. Ahead was a wall made of logs set on end in the ground. A large doorway in the wall allowed a view of several lodges. Smoke curled from their tops, and people moved among them.

Two men moved past the doorway, dressed alike in blue and white, with odd headdresses, also alike. They carried sticks that appeared harmless, but must be weapons of some sort.

As she moved closer, Star realized that these blue garments were not made of skins, but of some woven material like the blankets. *Aiee*, she thought, there is no end to the wonders here!

Three Owls spoke sharply to her and pointed to the left. They would not, it appeared, stay inside the enclosure formed by the log walls. Among the trees and stumps were scattered brush lean-to structures in all stages of disrepair. Some were occupied, some empty, some falling apart and being used as fuel by people camped nearby.

Three Owls poked around and finally chose one of the better shelters that was unoccupied.

"Here," he pointed, dropping his packs in the entrance.

"Find wood," he ordered in sign-talk. "Remember, if you run away, I will follow and kill you, very slowly."

Star nodded, frightened.

"I will bring firewood."

She quickly began to gather wood, deliberately

enough to be efficient, yet fast enough to avoid the
wrath of Three Owls.

She pondered what this place was called, and which
of the outside tribes it represented. *Fran-coy? Yen-
glees?* It mattered little, she supposed.

Then she saw it. Down the slope, through the trees,
the sparkling glitter of water. She moved in that direction, still picking up sticks from time to time. The
gentle slope fell away before her, down toward the
water, and she moved forward a few steps.

It was only then that Star realized the grandness of
the view before her. She was looking out across a
breathtaking body of water, a whole world of water, it
seemed. It had never occurred to her that earth's rim
itself could be made of water, meeting sky in the dim
blue of distance.

Odd ideas flitted through her head. What would
happen if one got into a canoe and paddled into the
world of water? Were there herds of water creatures
somewhere, like the buffalo herds of her own far
horizons?

She had an even stranger thought. When Sun Boy
dipped below earth's rim in the evening, would his
torch make the water hiss and boil, like cooking stones
dropped in the stew pit from the fire? Or if Sun Boy
rose from beyond the watery rim of this world, would
his torch be wet and difficult to light?

This must be *Mishi-ghan*, the first of the big-water
lakes mentioned by Traveler. These, he had said, were
fresh water.

Star was still standing in awestruck amazement when
she heard Three Owls calling. Frantically, she hurried
back up the slope, snatching sticks of firewood on the
way.

34

» » »

In the next day, Star observed many things. The village, she decided, belonged to the *Fran-coy*. They seemed to have no women of their own, though some lived with wives who were from local tribes.

Some, but not all, wore the blue-and-white garments made of woven material like blankets. Star decided they must be a warrior society, since they always carried weapons.

These weapons were of iron, the medicine stone that was now becoming familiar to her. She longed to hold one of the knives, knowing its medicine would give her strength, but the possibility seemed slim. She was watched too closely by her captor.

Three Owls did some trading, but it was apparent to her that he knew nothing of what he was doing. She watched him make several bad trades but did nothing to help him. If the man was stupid enough to trade foolishly, let him!

Several of the men cast admiring glances in her direction. Once she suspected that a man who came to trade attempted to buy her and was refused by Three Owls.

One man came more than once, and seemed more interested in Star than in trading.

"How are you called?" he asked her in sign-talk.

She glanced at Three Owls, but he was busy haggling over a trade involving some tobacco.

"Pale Star," she signed quickly.

The young man smiled, and his face was good to look at. The hair that surrounded it was dark and a little curly. She had noticed that many of the *Fran-coy* had curly hair. Among her own people, she now recalled, some of the family line of Heads Off had a slight curl to their hair, while most were straight.

Some of her relatives, too, had a slight fringe of fur on the face, too heavy to pluck with the clamshell tweezers. It was worn proudly, a sign of the blood of chiefs. This young man had a similar fringe along the jaw and upper lip.

But the most striking thing about the man was his eyes. Star had seen eyes of varying shades of brown, but these were a light gray-blue. Oddly, this did not appear to interfere with his vision.

He wore buckskins like those of the various tribes she saw represented around the fort. Somehow, though, there was much about him that resembled the outsiders.

"You are *Fran-coy*?" she asked, using the sign Traveler had taught her.

"My father. My mother is ———."

Here the young man used a sign unfamiliar to her.

"How is it?"

He repeated, then spoke the name of a tribe. She had heard this word before, but it meant nothing to her. There were many tribes here.

Three Owls turned and realized that the young man was talking to her. He spoke sharply, and the stranger spread his palms to protest innocence. After a short argument Three Owls turned back to his trading, and the other moved away. He glanced back at Star, who sat half in fear of what her captor would do. Even so, she risked one more question.

"How are you called?"

"Hunting Hawk. I will see you again."

"No," she started to protest, but Hunting Hawk was gone.

For the first time in many days, Star became optimistic. Here, she felt, was someone who could help her. He had shown no fear of Three Owls. It was like having the support of the unfortunate Winter Bear again, but much better. This man seemed quick and intelligent, and from the confident way he moved, she felt that he was a warrior of some skill.

Yes, he would defend her. He had told her he would see her again. She would be friendly to Hunting Hawk, gaining his interest and support, until she was able to bring about a release from Three Owls.

She did not delude herself. Release meant the death of Three Owls, because there would be no other way. She would kill him without hesitation, or Hunting Hawk could be persuaded to kill him in her defense. It would not matter.

At least now there was a person who cared. Even the brief contact gave her hope that, whatever his motives, Hunting Hawk would help her.

She turned back to watch Three Owls and the man he was haggling with. They were arguing mildly, the trade apparently already made, merely the final terms at issue.

The other man had spread several fine skins, and Three Owls was sorting them critically. Star wondered for a moment what Three Owls had of such value. Then an unpleasant suspicion struck her.

The man with the furs was looking at her covetously, his eyes roving over the smooth curves of her body. His half smile was almost a leer.

Surely Three Owls would not sell her. Yes, he might, she told herself.

The bargaining was now over, and Three Owls picked up a single fur he had selected. He turned to the girl and used sign-talk.

"You will be his for tonight," he told her with a sneer.

Star had never thought of this possibility. Three Owls intended to use her to sell to others repeatedly for a short while. There was no such custom among her people, and her skin crawled at the prospect.

She thought rapidly. Her reaction was of utmost importance now. She tried to appear calm and matter-of-fact, though her heart was pounding in her ears.

"Of course," she replied coolly, "but I am unclean!"

It was true. She had noted the heavy feeling of approaching menses for the past few days, and she had begun only this morning.

The other man cried out accusingly at Three Owls and snatched back his otter skin. Three Owls loudly protested his innocence and turned a black look at Star.

"You said nothing until now," he signed angrily.

"I did not know," the girl signed back, spreading her palms in helpless consternation.

The other man stamped away in anger, carrying his furs.

Star realized that this relief was only temporary. In a few days she would have to face the entire scene again. She wondered why Three Owls had not struck at her in anger. It must be that he was afraid to touch her. Yes, he was afraid of her uncleanness.

Now a new plan began to emerge. She could use this situation to her advantage. In fact, very quickly she had formed in her mind the outlines of a complicated scheme. The timing must be exactly right, and the right people must be present.

She smiled to herself for the first time in many days.

35

» » »

Star knew that she must plan her strategy carefully as well as quickly. She had only a few days to do so.

It was a welcome relief to be spared the attentions of Three Owls. She was isolated in a small shelter a few steps from his. This gave her a bit of freedom that she had not had since the loss of Traveler. At the thought of Traveler, her heart became heavy again. He had never been properly mourned, and she regretted that circumstances had made it impossible. Nevertheless, she would plan carefully, a plan that would have made Traveler proud of her.

Her plan consisted of two parts. One was to cultivate the friendship of Hunting Hawk. That was not difficult. The young man was already interested. She must, however, be sure that he was interested enough to come to her aid. She hoped that he was more adept at combat than Winter Bear. Of course, Bear had had no warning, no suspicion that his cousin would behave in so deadly a manner. Hunting Hawk would be forewarned. She would be sure to inform him of the danger, and he could back off if he preferred. Somehow, though, she did not think he would be one to retreat.

The other part of the plan involved extremely close observation of Three Owls. She must see what he did with his weapons, where he laid them down, where he placed them while not wearing them. She must be able to see in advance every action of this unpredictable man.

She had been too preoccupied with self-defense and survival to observe much until now. However, with the relative freedom of her withdrawal to the menstrual lodge, she could observe Three Owls more closely. She watched his habits. Even though he was unpredictable, she began to see his manner of doing things.

Three Owls' favorite weapon, she observed, was the throwing ax. It could be used while held in the hand, but it could also be thrown with deadly effect, as she had witnessed. It would be the one.

Hunting Hawk, meanwhile, seemed only too eager to cooperate. The man appeared to be a loner, living alone in a semipermanent lodge near the gate of the stockade. She learned that he was employed as a scout for the *Fran-coy.*

Star found opportunity to encounter him as she gathered firewood or brought water from the lake. At first a smile or a nod established contact. Then she began sign-talk. That was not always easy, when her hands were occupied with carrying.

"Be careful," she warned him. "Three Owls will be angry."

"If I talk to you?"

She nodded.

"You are his wife?"

Star paused. She had not thought of it in this way. High regard for marriage was held by the People, and her feelings for it had been good during her growing up. Now, she must concede that she was, in effect, the wife of the crazed Three Owls. Her upbringing made her hesitate to admit it.

"His captive," she answered.

Her downcast eyes told Hunting Hawk her story.

"Run away?"

"No, he will kill me."

He nodded in understanding.

Star stooped to pick up sticks, and the young man moved on as if they had had no contact.

"We will talk later," he signed.

The girl's optimism was returning. She could see her plan working. Already, Hunting Hawk was sympathetic. She must make him more so. One risk of her scheme was the attitude of Hunting Hawk. It was possible that he might think a wife should be beaten occasionally. If she set up a confrontation, expecting help from him, what if she then discovered that he thought her beating well deserved?

She did not think this would be the case, but she must be absolutely certain.

At their next meeting, the young man smiled and greeted her pleasantly.

"You must be careful," she warned again. "Three Owls is dangerous. He killed one man for trying to help me."

The look of indignant anger on Hunting Hawk's face showed Star that she was reading him correctly. That was enough for now.

"I must go."

She hurried away, well aware that the young man would have prolonged the conversation.

Meanwhile, as she moved around the camping spot of Three Owls, she continued to make certain of his attitude. She must know more about the menstrual taboos of his tribe.

Three Owls certainly did not object to her carrying wood for the fire. However, he had made it clear that she was not to touch his food. That was common in many tribes, she knew. He even refused to use drinking water that she had carried.

He avoided physical contact completely. Star assumed that this avoidance must also extend to his weapons, but she must be absolutely sure. She remembered her conversation, now long ago, when Plum Leaf had warned her about touching tools or weapons. Perhaps she could talk to another woman.

Near the path to the lake, she had noticed a small shelter occupied by a young woman. She stepped aside and approached the woman on her next trip for water.

Star gave the sign for greeting.

"You are unclean, too?" she began.

"Yes," nodded the other girl, "come in."

Again Star felt the bond of sisterhood.

"How are you called?"

"I am Pale Star. You?"

"Dove Woman. Your man is Three Owls?"

Star nodded reluctantly.

"You know Three Owls?"

"Only a little. He has been here before. It is said he has a new woman."

Star did not reply.

"He has a cousin—White Bear?"

"Winter Bear," corrected Star, before she thought.

It would be best to say little about that, she decided.

"Winter Bear is not here," she continued vaguely.

The other girl seemed satisfied.

"Is Three Owls of your tribe?" Star questioned.

"No, but they are allies. You are not from this region."

It was a statement, not a question.

"No. I am a captive."

Dove Woman nodded. On her face was a mixture of sympathy and mild distrust. Captive women, especially attractive ones, were sometimes objects of jealousy and dislike. That this girl was willing to be friendly indicated that her own marriage was secure.

"Where are your people?"

"Far away, west across the Big River. They are called Elk-dog People."

Dove Woman nodded again.

"Tell me, sister," Star probed a bit further, "I do not

know of the menstrual customs here. I am not to touch his food or his person. What else?"

The young woman smiled.

"Touch nothing, especially weapons. They will never be good again. Is it not so among your people?"

"Not so much. Some tribes in our country, more than others."

It was difficult to restrain her satisfaction. She had been correct in her assumption. Three Owls was afraid of her touch. Afraid for himself and for his weapons.

She rose to depart.

"I must go. Three Owls will wonder where I am."

Dove Woman smiled sympathetically.

"We will talk again. You must tell me of your Horse People."

Star smiled and nodded.

"And you must tell me more of how it is here."

She hurried away, smiling to herself.

36

Hunting Hawk sat with his back against a tree and watched the girl. Pale Star, she called herself. From the time he first saw her, he had been attracted to her.

It had bothered him somewhat that she was with Three Owls. No self-respecting woman would be in the company of that one by choice. And that, of course, proved to be the answer. She was a captive, miserable with her lot.

His heart went out to the girl. He thought at first of trying to buy her, but no, someone had tried that, it was said. Three Owls was only interested in selling her for a night at a time.

Well, there was little that he, Hunting Hawk, could do about that. If the girl belonged to Three Owls, he could do so if he wished. Still, it bothered Hawk.

Several things bothered him about this situation. He knew Three Owls, though not well, from previous contacts. The man had always been considered strange, cruel, and sadistic. Hunting Hawk wondered how he had come to possess the girl. Surely, there was more to the story than was apparent.

Then there was the matter of the cousin. Winter Bear, he had been called. He had always been a constant companion of Three Owls, until now. Where was Winter Bear? No one had ventured to question Three Owls in detail, and he had been very vague about his cousin's whereabouts.

Someone had asked the girl, it was said, and had received an equally vague answer, that the cousin was not with them. That, of course, could be easily seen.

Hunting Hawk, however, was quick to make excuses for the girl in his own mind. She was evasive in her answers, he believed, because she was afraid of the wrath of Three Owls. She must live in constant fear.

Even Hunting Hawk was astonished, however, at the way his heart went out to her. Just to look at the big sad eyes made him want to hold and protect her. He worried a little about what his reaction would be if he chanced to be present when Pale Star was mistreated. It would be very difficult to remain uninvolved.

The girl herself was doing nothing to ease this problem. She appeared attracted to him. Her sad-sweet smile reached out to him in a helpless appeal, a cry for assistance. Yet, all the while, she kept warning him of the wrath of Three Owls.

Hawk suspected that she might be using him. Actually, he did not care. He was somewhat flattered by the fact that he was her choice to ask for assistance. For that was surely what was implied.

He might have resented her for this. He had no use for women who tried to cause trouble by manipulating men. There were some who made little pretense, rutting with any willing male like a dog in season.

Perhaps this was the difference he saw in the eyes of Pale Star. She was frightened, confused, and helpless. Her very spirit reached out to him.

To be sure, he had had some doubts. There was a time when he had been faced with a decision. He must either turn away and forget the girl or convince himself that he would hold back nothing in his efforts to help her. The sensible thing, of course, was to back away. There were many unanswered questions here. Sometimes he thought he could do that. He planned a scouting trip, to take him away for a few days, so that he might feel less of the pressure of decision.

That might have been successful, had he been able to do it. However, before he was ready to depart, another factor intruded. A party, coming in from the southwest, had discovered a body on the trail, two sleeps out. That in itself was not unusual. There were other circumstances.

The victim was recognized by the travelers as Winter Bear, kinsman to Three Owls. He lay on his back, with a wound in his forehead that might have been made by an ax. Supplies and trade goods were strewn around in disarray, indicating a hurried looting of the victim's packs. There was no sign of a struggle, but the dead man had been scalped.

When the newly arrived travelers learned that Three Owls was at the fort, they went to give the sad news. Three Owls' reaction had been remarkable, to say the least. It was bound to come, he told them philosophically, given Bear's well-known tendency to make trouble. He had not seen his cousin, he informed them, for three, no, four moons, while on a trip down the Big River. They had quarreled and separated.

There were many who questioned this story, or parts of it. Hunting Hawk was very suspicious. He was almost certain that he had noticed a fresh scalp curing in the smoke of their campfire on Three Owls' first night here. Could the man actually have murdered his own cousin? Stranger things had happened.

This certainly could account for the anxiety, the evasiveness, of the girl. And if there was any truth to his suspicion, she could be in real danger. A madman capable of killing his own kinsman would kill a captive without hesitation if it pleased him.

Hunting Hawk emptied his pack and changed his plans. He would stay near, to try to protect the girl.

He hoped that the soldiers would not want him to go on a scout in the next few days. He would have to refuse and could tell no one why. Ah, well, it mattered little. He was already considered a little odd. His mixed blood made him a curiosity.

The father of Hunting Hawk had died before he was born. Not in battle, but in an accident. His mother had told him the story many times. The tree they were felling caught a shift of wind in its top and toppled the wrong way. But, she always told the child, his father was a great warrior. Hunting Hawk must live to make his father proud.

Hawk wondered now what she would think of this turn of events. She had died three winters ago, disappointed that her son had not chosen a wife. That was when he left her tribe to go west with the soldiers.

He shifted his position slightly so that he could see better. Through the trees he could watch the area where Three Owls camped and observe the movements of the girl. He attempted to avoid the appearance of watching her, but he really did not care what anyone thought.

Now he saw Pale Star approaching from the woods to his left. Perhaps if he decided to walk down to the lake, he would encounter her, and there could be a short conversation. He did not see Three Owls but knew that he was lying in the shade of the brush shelter.

Hunting Hawk rose and walked in that direction, apparently in an aimless fashion.

There was no premonition, no warning that things were about to burst into flame like dry tinder. Hawk misjudged his pace slightly, or maybe the girl was hurrying just a little. At any rate, she reached Three Owls' dwelling before Hunting Hawk approached. Hawk was certain that she saw him, but she made no sign of recognition.

Instead, she did a most incredible thing. In full view of Three Owls, the girl stooped to pick up his throwing ax and toss it aside. Then she dumped her armful of wood where the ax had been.

She should have known, Hawk's thoughts shouted

into his head, not to touch the weapon. Now Three Owls would be crazed with fury. If his suspicions were correct, the madman might kill the girl just for such a blunder. Hawk dashed forward.

Three Owls came bursting out of the shelter, screaming with rage. The girl dropped to her knees, terrified. Ignoring the risk of her uncleanness, the man rushed at her and struck her hard across the side of the head with his hand, knocking her to the dust. Three Owls turned and grasped his tainted ax and whirled back toward the whimpering girl. She threw up a hand to deflect the expected blow.

"Stop!" shouted Hunting Hawk as he sprinted forward.

Three Owls turned to face the newcomer.

"She meant no harm," began Hawk. "She did not know—"

He stopped short, recognition dawning on him like a flash of real-fire. The girl *did* know, and had set up the incident in the hope that Hawk would protect her. Anger flooded over him at the thought that he had been used.

But there was no time now to think of that. Three Owls was coming forward, all the pent-up frustrations of past days showing plainly in his face. He said nothing, but madness blazed in his eyes. He was beyond all reason.

Hunting Hawk reached for the knife at his waist. It was a poor defense against a throwing ax, but he had no alternative. With resignation, he determined to do his best.

He had no other choice. Even if he abandoned the girl now, as she probably deserved, Three Owls would be determined to kill him.

37

›› ›› ››

Pale Star lay in the dust and watched the scene develop. Three Owls circled, balancing his ax for the fight. The girl realized, too late, that she had put Hunting Hawk at a decided disadvantage. He was armed only with his knife, and Three Owls, mad with rage, had both his throwing ax and the knife at his waist.

Worse yet, Star felt that Hunting Hawk had unquestionably saved her life. In return, she had placed him in extreme peril. She scrambled to her feet.

The two men circled, neither willing to attempt the first blow. Hawk feinted and dodged back out of reach.

Now they had moved around so that Hawk's back was toward the girl. She looked past him at the blazing anger in Three Owls' face. It was, perhaps, her fascination with that face that allowed her to see the throw coming.

Three Owls squared his stance, stood swaying for balance only the space of a heartbeat, and then the deadly ax shot forward.

She had lived this scene before, watched with horror as the ax described its whirling flight to administer the death blow to Winter Bear.

"Look out!" she screamed.

Neither of the combatants could understand the shout in the language of the People, but both heard. It may have been that this distraction spoiled the throw, or that a tainted weapon does not fly true. Whatever the cause, the whirling blade brushed past the head of Hunting Hawk, flashed on past Star, and struck with a solid "thunk" into the trunk of a tree behind her.

Three Owls did not hesitate. He leaped forward, drawing his knife as he did so, and the two clashed.

Each grasped the wrist of the other, the knife-wielding right hand, and they struggled in balanced combat. Locked in a deadly dance, they swayed and circled, neither able to gain an advantage. They tried to trip, kick, knee the groin, but neither could accomplish it.

Star stood staring, realizing that her life might well depend on the outcome of the struggle.

In the shifting, pushing dance of death, something must eventually break the rhythm. The break came in the form of a small, round stone. Star saw it on the ground under the feet of the men, a stone hardly bigger than the acorns of her own country.

It rolled under the foot of Hunting Hawk, his ankle twisted, and he fell heavily. His knife clattered from his fist, and he was unarmed.

Three Owls was quick to gain his advantage, rolling astride his stunned opponent. Hawk had retained his grasp on the wrist that held the knife and frantically held on against hope, trying to prevent the thrust of the blade.

Hunting Hawk now began to think that the end was near. His strength was failing, and that of the madman astride his waist seemed to be increasing. He saw the shining point come trembling, nearer his throat. The end was only a few heartbeats away.

Then he felt, rather than heard, the impact of a blow. A convulsive shudder ran through the wiry muscles of Three Owls, and then the limbs went slack. The burning eyes reflected a moment of surprise, then only blankness, as the dying man collapsed in a limp heap.

Exhausted, Hunting Hawk could scarcely push his opponent's body aside. He had not even freed himself yet when he saw the girl, eyes wide with shock, standing over the tangled combatants. In her hand she held the throwing ax that Three Owls would never throw again.

Hunting Hawk rolled free and stood, swaying with exhaustion.

"You saved my life," he said in sign-talk.

"And you, mine."

They stared at each other a little while. People were running toward them.

Star could hardly believe it was over. The ax in her hand dropped unnoticed to the ground.

Hunting Hawk was explaining to the crowd, in a tongue she did not understand. There were gasps of astonishment. Hawk turned to her, and asked a question in sign-talk.

"Tell me, did he kill his cousin?"

Star nodded, through tears of relief. There was a murmur around the circle, and nods of sympathy. It seemed that these people had had little use for the ill-tempered Three Owls.

The excitement over, the crowd began to melt away. Pale Star and Hunting Hawk stood facing each other, still numb from the intensity of the incident. Hunting Hawk glanced at the still form on the ground.

"You want the scalp?"

She shook her head.

He stepped over and picked up his knife and the one Three Owls had dropped. He sheathed his own and handed the other to her.

"Take this. It is yours. You killed him."

The haft of the medicine knife fit comfortably into her palm. She could feel its strength. She still could hardly believe that she had killed a man, but she saw no way it could have been avoided.

"I risked your life," she signed.

"It is nothing. You saved it, too."

He smiled.

"How is it that you were with him?"

He indicated the limp form.

"He killed my father and captured me."

She saw no need to go into the intricacies of Traveler's identity and her relationship to him.

"I am sorry. What now?"

"I do not know."

"You have much property," he indicated the packs in Three Owls' shelter.

Star had not even thought of that.

"I must think. I need some time."

Hawk nodded.

"I will be here when you need me."

"Why?"

"I want you to be my woman."

There was a moment of panic as she realized the import of this statement. It was possible, even, that this man thought of her now as his property.

Hawk saw the alarm on her face.

"No, no," he protested. "When you are ready, we will talk about it."

His friendly smile removed much of her apprehension. She was able to return the smile.

"It is good," she signed. "Later, we will talk."

Author's Note

With the previous volumes in this series, readers have asked about the geographic locations mentioned. Since *Pale Star* covers a large area, it may be well to orient the course of their travels.

The book begins in the tallgrass region of what is now central Kansas, the home of "the People." Drought forces them to migrate south and east, and Star is carried a captive to the Ozark country of southern Missouri and Arkansas.

The trek northward follows the Mississippi and its tributaries, then finally overland to the area of the Great Lakes. During this time period the French and English were maneuvering for control of the territory, producing an unsettled political situation such as that described. The French are known to have established outposts near the southern end of Lake Michigan.

There were apparently wandering traders, as depicted in "Traveler," exchanging commodities among many tribes.

As in previous volumes, no specific tribes are men-

tioned, to avoid preconceived ideas. The reader may
feel that he or she recognizes some groups. That is
good, because it indicates that we have succeeded in
making the story real.

Don Coldsmith

GENEALOGY

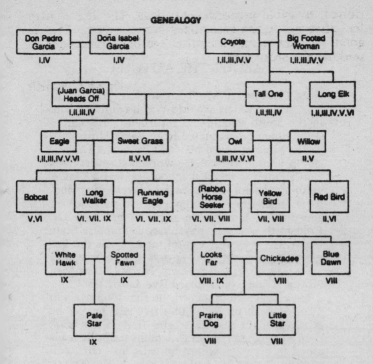

Dates for Volumes in the Spanish Bit Saga

I	TRAIL OF THE SPANISH BIT	—	1540-44
II	BUFFALO MEDICINE	—	1559-61
III	THE ELK-DOG HERITAGE	—	1544-45
IV	FOLLOW THE WIND	—	1547-48
V	MAN OF THE SHADOWS	—	1565-66
VI	DAUGHTER OF THE EAGLE	—	1583-84
VII	MOON OF THUNDER	—	1600-01
VIII	THE SACRED HILLS	—	1625-27
IX	PALE STAR	—	1630-31

Dates are only approximate, since the People have no written calendar.

Volume II, BUFFALO MEDICINE, is out of chronological order, and should appear between Volumes IV and V.

Characters in the Genealogy appear in the volumes indicated.

ABOUT THE AUTHOR

DON COLDSMITH was born in Iola, Kansas, in 1926. He served as a World War II combat medic in the South Pacific and returned to his native state where he graduated from Baker University in 1949 and received his M.D. from the University of Kansas in 1958. He worked at several jobs before entering medical school: he was a YMCA group counselor, a gunsmith, a taxidermist, and, for a short time, a Congregational preacher. In addition to his private medical practice, Dr. Coldsmith is a staff physician at Emporia State University's Health Center, teaches in the English Department, and is active as a freelance writer, lecturer, and rancher. He and his wife of 26 years, Edna, have raised five daughters.

Dr. Coldsmith produced the first ten novels in "The Spanish Bit Saga" in a five-year period; he writes and revises the stories first in his head, then in longhand. From this manuscript he reads aloud to his wife, whom he calls his "chief editor." Finally the finished version is skillfully typed by his longtime office receptionist.

Of his decision to create, or re-create, the world of the Plains Indian in the 16h and 17th centuries, the author says: "There has been very little written about this time period. I wanted also to portray these Native Americans as human beings, rather than as stereotyped 'Indians.' That word does not appear anywhere in the series—for a reason. As I have researched the time and place, the indigenous cultures, it's been a truly inspiring experience for me."